River Sisters

The Giver

Jan Dearman

BEACON
PUBLISHING GROUP

For information, or to order additional copies, please contact:

Beacon Publishing Group
P.O. Box 41573 Charleston, S.C. 29423
800.817.8480| beaconpublishinggroup.com

Publisher's catalog available by request.

ISBN-13: 978-1-949472-71-4

ISBN-10: 1-949472-71-4

Published in 2019. Printed in the USA.

First Edition. New York, NY 10001.

May 1838

Nancy raised her head from the interminable procession of stitches—short, evenly spaced, an indiscernible seam in the fine, blue silk of the gown. Rubbing and stretching the taut muscles of her neck and smoothing wisps of hair back into her bun, she presented her face to the sun, now thrusting its arms across the porch to caress her high bronze cheekbones. So many days she had longed for such warmth—days when her blood seemed frozen like the deep winter river, and nights when only three blankets and the cocoon of David's arms could ease her shivering. She was a child of spring and sang with the valley the song of rebirth. There had been no cold since the melting of last March's snow; this year the valley sang an early song, and it lulled her unborn child to sleep in the stillness of his mother's womb.

With only the slightest mound beneath the trim waist of her gray homespun, Nancy rose to her feet, lay the material on the quilt of the nearby rocker, and descended the puncheon steps of the two-story log cabin. The sun was making its descent across the sky, against which David's corn would soon be rising, tall and straight and golden—the tassels blowing in the breeze like the hair of a thousand maidens cavorting along the riverbank. Already, the crop was knee-high, the bean plants inching up the poles. The shocks would be dry and lifeless and the harvest stored for winter by the time of birth.

This child would be a child of winter. He would covet the purity of the snow blanket, as it draped thick folds over the shoulders of the mountain mothers. As he sprang through the forest with the strength of the deer, he would glory in breath clouds, puffing like smoke from his strong lungs. He would break the heavy icicles suspended from rock ledges and throw them like arrows at a gray squirrel, who would scurry away and scold from the safety of his tree.

Nancy smiled within herself—would a girl child be any less daring? She had followed her brothers with a heart burning for adventure, until the time of play was ended. Then the path of the child divided—her brothers going the way of the brave, and she, the womanly way of encampment and healing. An ember of yearning for their freedom and proving still smoldered within her, but she had become a proficient cook, a knowledgeable healer, and the finest seamstress outside New Echota. The crops she and her husband tended grew in rows as even as her stitches; the garden patches, as perfect as the squares she pieced and quilted. These skills she had brought to David; because of him, she felt great joy and thankfulness that the Giver had brought her forth as a woman.

Nancy pulled the woolen shawl around her shoulders as she walked toward the river, into the lengthening rays of sun. The river curved around the point of land given to them by her father. Good land—deep, dark, rich soil. The mountains behind them gave them meat, the river gave them fish, their crops were abundant, and the income from her needlework made them almost prosperous. Their life was "blessed," as the preacher at the mission would say.

She was reminded of the psalm she had read in recent days: "As arrows are in the hand of a mighty man; so are children of the youth. Happy is the man that hath his quiver full of them." David was a mighty man—a very somber man in recent months. Yet this child had brought a smile to his lips, when, for so long, there had been no song in his soul. Would this child's heart be rent from the sky, the wind, the water of the valley? Would his hair grow gray and his eyes dim, and would his corrupted shell be laid to rest one day in the hallowed soil of this land, leaving his soul to soar above the clouds with the ancient ones? These questions haunted David, her husband, a mighty man whose spirit groaned with anger, sorrow, and frustration.

The treachery of the Ridgites and the threatened removal of their people were the talk of the landing store. She saw a hunger for blood in David's eyes at the mention of Jackson's name, and she struggled to see beyond her comfort and joy to understand. They had been one with the land for a thousand years—would the Giver allow the names of a few traitors on a piece of paper to tear them from their heritage since the beginning of time?

Nancy positioned herself on the boulder near the poplar on the bank and watched David's skiff bobbing from its mooring. This time of year, the rock should be covered by floodwater, but the spring's gentle rains had given the earth only adequate moisture for early crops. Nancy looked across the river at the mountains surrounding their land like a huddle of old grandmothers, chanting over the new life in her body: give him the strength of the bear, the heart of the panther, the feet of the deer, and the eyes and soul of the eagle—to see the smallest creature in the field and to soar high in the clouds between God and man.

She closed her eyes and felt the breeze stirring her lashes and the wisps of hair around her face. A murmur of voices in the air came to her sensitive ears, then, the creaking of wagon wheels and the sound of horses' hooves plodding along the river trace. She turned to face the wind and waited for life to follow sound. She scanned the horizon toward Ross's Landing. She felt only the constriction of her heart and the drumbeat of pulse at her temple. Rising from her position on the river rock, she stood to face the cabin. Men and horses were coming, the Jenkins boy driving his father's ox cart. She moved toward the house—her feet, slow, deliberate and sure, belaying her runaway heart.

She had reached the corner of the corn field, when she turned toward the sound of David's voice: "Nancy, no!" He was running toward her from the trees, and his new face frightened her. She remembered he had taken his English name from the story told him at the mission: a young brave, strong and fearless, killed a lion and a bear, because he had been given the heart of the lion and the bear. David's face was not the face he had worn into the forest this morning; it was the face of the creature trembling in terror and panic before the kill. In a few heartbeats, he stood before her, his shoulders glistening with perspiration, the smell of earth and fresh kill upon his sun-warmed skin.

Nancy watched over David's shoulder, as the leader with the broad-brimmed hat reigned his horse away from the other blue uniforms. The saber at the man's side slapped the saddle, as his mount halted before them with a huffing snort. "I am Captain Dickerson. I must inform you that the period for your voluntary emigration from this land has expired. Under order of United States General Winfield Scott, I must now oversee your removal to join your brethren in the far West."

Eyes piercing the depths of the captain's blue eyes, David stood rigid, bow in hand, a string of squirrels over his shoulder. Like a mother hen tucking her chick under her wing, David's only movement was to wrap his free arm around the fullness of Nancy's skirt, to pull her behind him.

The captain raised a gloved hand and motioned to the men behind him. Three of them dismounted. They carried rifles with long knife blades attached to the muzzles. Nancy drew close to David. She felt the heat of her breath and the painful throbbing and swelling of fear in her chest.

The men surrounded them, weapons drawn. Nancy felt the gentle press of the bayonet against her back and flinched. With a cry for blood, David lunged for the captain's horse, which reared and threatened to eject its rider. The soldier at David's side rammed his rifle butt against David's head, felling him like a tree. Nancy's heart burst, as she covered her husband with her body, her tears dampening his vest.

Moaning and dazed, David struggled to push himself to his knees and sought Nancy's shoulder. The officer who had struck him reached under David's arm. Had he the strength, David would have torn him with his teeth.

"There is no use resisting," the captain declared, reigning his mount. "Load yourselves in the cart. You may gather what possessions you can carry. The rest will be collected and brought to you in a couple of days." The captain jerked his head back toward the cabin. "Put him in the wagon. She can see to their belongings." Through eyes filled with tears of anger and hatred, as well as fear, Nancy watched the captain turn his horse toward the trail, with the parting directive: "Make sure you disarm him." He spurred his horse to a gallop—perhaps, back toward the stockade—the stockade her people had thought would never be used.

"Ma'am, I'm Private Burnett. Let me help you with your husband."

For the first time, Nancy noticed the face of the man in blue to her right. The sympathy and kindness she saw in his eyes made her want to claw them. If he felt so much concern for the inhumanity of their treatment, for the helplessness of their situation, why did he not move to defend them? She spat at his feet.

Ignoring her disdain, the private took Nancy's elbows, lifted her to her feet, and set her aside as if she were porcelain. He advised, "Ma'am, you'd best see about your things." Assisting the other soldier, the private knelt, wrapped David's arm around his neck, and carried him. The third soldier, bayonet still at ready, remained with Nancy, who watched as her husband was half-carried, half-dragged toward the waiting wagon.

Nancy turned to look at the soldier behind her. With the bayonet, he gestured toward the cabin. Nancy glared into the man's eyes and growled, in Tsalagi, the gravest of curses. She then straightened her back, squared her shoulders, and proceeded toward the cabin. The men in blue might strip them of their heritage and steal from them their home, but they could not taint the color of their blood, the nobility of their character. Their big knives were no match for the long, gleaming, razor-edged blade of hatred sheathed in her soul. Their big knives could only pierce the body—at worst, setting the spirit free. Hatred could do so much more.

As Nancy passed the ox cart, she noticed Sam Jenkins—a sloven with his narrow shoulders slumped, head lowered, eyes cast down on the weathered boots at the end of scrawny ankles showing three inches below his pants. A runt—a pitiful, pockmarked creature who, had he been a Cherokee of old, might have sacrificed himself for the sake of purity and beauty.

On the bed of the cart, David, holding his head, slumped against a bag of corn flour she recognized as having come from their larder. As she proceeded up the porch and into the door, another man in blue bumped her aside. He was carrying a basket containing canned goods from the shelves above her wood stove.

What should she take with her? At this point, everything seemed dear, yet nothing seemed as precious as her injured husband. Her bag—she must get her handbag—a large tanned deer hide pouch, expertly beaded. David had given it to her as a wedding gift. Nancy climbed the stairs to the sleeping loft. Tears trickled from the corners of her eyes as she gazed upon the marriage bed where her child had been conceived.

The child! She must think of the child! From the clothes peg on the wall, Nancy took her handbag and stuffed into it the money she had tucked behind a log in the gable. From the cedar chest, she took a small blanket of the softest weave she had stored for the baby. She added to the purse several handkerchiefs for David's wound and the silver etui he had bought from a trader at the landing store. She drew the leather strings, backed down the ladder, and scoured the main floor. She placed David's pipe and tobacco pouch in her sewing basket, along with as many dried medicinal herbs as it would hold.

Hat in hand, Private Burnett hesitated at the door. "Ma'am, the sergeant says it's time to go. He says they'll be bringing the rest to you later."

Nancy knew this was not true. Vultures circled, prepared to swoop down on the remains of their life. She would not have them feed on the parts closest to the heart, those still warm with love, memory—or hope. She draped the baby blanket over her shoulder and exited the door, stopping long enough to retrieve the blue gown from the rocker and the quilt for David. The deerskin purse hung from her wrist, hidden beneath the dress and cover. Picking up the sewing basket, Nancy proceeded down the steps to the ox cart, where she placed their possessions on the wagon bed near David's feet. From her purse, she took one of the clean handkerchiefs, folded just as David would have it, ready for the pocket of his Sunday coat.

He always looked so handsome—the black wool sharp against the crisp, white, starched collar, framing the bronze ruggedness of his face. He stood at least a head taller than she; by his side, she felt sheltered and relished her femininity. Wearing hair and dress in the latest fashion of the whites, her own native features refined by a touch of their ancestral blood, Nancy knew she and David were an attractive mating and would produce fine offspring, strong and comely.

She touched the cloth of memory to her face before returning to the porch to wet it in the water bucket. The water was cool and clean; she splashed her face and smoothed the loose strands of hair from her eyes.

Hitching up her skirt, Nancy sprang up next to her husband in the wagon. She covered him with the quilt he had worn around his shoulders during the last snow. He had sat in the rocker on the porch in the deep chill of winter and had watched, entranced and reverent, as their valley became a white cocoon—pure, silent, still. Within the embrace of winter, the peace and contentment of seasoned fires, their child had begun to grow.

Nancy's eyes brimmed with tears of loss and anger. She brushed her dress sleeve across her face, as she filled the handkerchief with slippery elm bark from her basket and held it against the swelling on David's head.

"Private Burnett!" she summoned.

"Ma'am?" He looked shocked at the sound of her voice.

"Mind fetching me that water bucket and ladle up here?"

"No, ma'am." The lackey seemed eager to attend to her request and placed the bucket over the side of the wagon.

Picking up the blue silk gown, she asked Burnett, "You have a wife?"

Surprised, Burnett replied, "Yes, ma'am—married almost a year."

Nancy thrust the dress into his chest. "Give her this. Tell her this is what savage women do when they are not grinding corn in a tree stump!"

* * * * * * * * *

In Nancy's lap, their unborn child cradled his father's head, as the cart bumped and swayed over rocky patches and sank and sloshed in ruts where shadowed earth had held the moisture of late snow and early rain. They were nearing the landing store, when Nancy realized they had joined a disorganized procession of people, possessions, and military personnel converging on the hill near Gardener's farm. Rising to her knees and laying David's head on the baby's blanket, Nancy observed the confluence of emigrants—on mules or horses laden with bulging flour sacks and saddlebags—on wagons, heavy with household goods, occasionally a chair perched atop the precarious pile like a watchtower—in fine carriages, with valises stacked orderly within the roof railing—on foot, their valuables dragged on sleds, or toted in baskets and pouches that curved their backs and pulled their limbs to the ground. Many had children in tow, some, infants in back slings. Several, like her, carried new life into the uncertain future.

Some youngsters, innocent and excited, scampered and frolicked as if on a glorious adventure. They would be unaware until night came, when they lay before a strange fire in the confines of the stockade and observed, in silence, the tears of their mothers and the fear, so foreign in their fathers' eyes.

Sam Jenkins tugged the lead of the ox and brought it to a halt before the stockade, a structure of pickets made of split trees and sharpened to points, set in the ground around an arrangement of cabins for the soldiers and stables for their horses.

"David, we're at the stockade." Nancy knelt beside her husband and helped him rise to a sitting position. She knew his head was pounding and his vision clouded, but she willed her strength into his body and mind. She was afraid. His heart had been tested; she needed him to lead them into this thick, dark forest, where no man's foot had broken path.

David scooted himself to the edge of the wagon bed. Holding Nancy's poultice to his head, he watched the conflux of people merging into the gate. Some he recognized as neighbors, a few relatives—mixed bloods, whole bloods, eyes downcast, or seeking the eyes of blue coats to make silent oaths of hatred and revenge.

Nancy alighted from the cart and gathered their remaining possessions. "Put your weight on me." She gave her shoulder to her husband.

David grasped her arm and turned her toward him. He stroked her brow, tracing the line of her forehead, her cheek, then cupped her chin in the broad, rough nest of his hand. He looked at her through the fog of pain and sorrow, as if to etch in his soul the memory of her face and to channel into her the strength of the lion and of the bear. He frightened her, as she knew this moment of anguish and love would drive her days and haunt her nights forevermore.

Their encampment was like many scattered about the interior of the enclosure: little movement save for the occasional stoking and stirring of the pools of light and memory amidst the still, cold visages. Their fire was strong, the flame high, but it failed to ease the chill of the icy stream coursing through Nancy's body. David sat propped against the trunk of a tree. Its height had been seized and hewn into pickets for the stockade. No longer tall and wide with sheltering arms outstretched for man and beast, its base now remained to offer what it could—support for David's weary, weakened back. Nancy lay in the cradle of her husband's arm, his head reclined on hers, as visions of the past and shadows of the future danced before them in the crackling, snapping fingers of light.

In the early dawning of this day, Nancy had stirred the fires of their hearth and had sat before the flame in the pacific solitude of one whose life was complete, secure. In the dim light of morning, her deft fingers had moved along the seam of the silk, as if by instinct—their traces straight and orderly as the days of her life.

Now the flames laughed, spitting, hissing—but still in the bounds of their fire circle. The blue silk was gone; but the mind that had envisioned it, the hands that had patterned and cut it, and the fingers that had stitched it were still strong. The West was not their land, but there they must make a new home for themselves and for their child.

Nancy's trance was interrupted by the muffled sobs of a child—not the babies' cries of hunger or discomfort that had punctuated the rumblings of the camp, but a child's choking on tears of sadness and fear.

Nancy held David's head as she moved away from his shoulder. Folding the baby blanket with her free hand, she made a pillow for him and covered him with the quilt they had shared.

Following the sound, Nancy rounded the corner of the nearby stable and found a young girl, huddled and shivering under the remnant of a feed sack. Her face was hidden against her arms, folded and propped on her knees.

Nancy stooped beside her and asked in Tsalagi, "Where is your mother?"

The girl recoiled in fear. Sweeping away her tears, she assessed Nancy before responding in English, "My mother is dead from my birth."

Nancy realized there was room in her heart for more pain and continued, "Where is your father?"

The girl hid her face in the valley of skirt between her knees. Her reply was muffled, "I have not seen him since he went into the forest this morning."

Nancy brushed away the tears coursing her cheeks. "What is your name?"

The girl raised her head. "Sara—Sara Colaquee."

Nancy directed, "Come, Sara Colaquee. Join my husband and me at our fire. You will be warm."

Sara stared at Nancy for several seconds, then nodded.

Nancy folded the remnant of sacking as a cushion for the sleepy child's head. "Lie down, Sara, and rest," she commanded with a mother's gentleness.

Sara, empty and fatigued, acquiesced. Nancy covered her with her shawl, then joined her sleeping husband. Slipping herself under the quilt beside David, she wrapped his arm around her middle and relished the weight and warmth of him against her.

Sara's face was lighted by the fire's glow. How old, Nancy wondered—six, maybe seven or eight? Her cheeks still held the soft roundness of a babe, but her arms and legs were as sleek and strong as a young colt. Thoughts of her own child in such a situation brought fresh tears, but she determined to care for this child with the love and compassion she would want for her own. If her child ever found himself alone, perhaps the Almighty would remember her kindness and provide a caretaker for him. She fell asleep with the words of petition on her lips.

Nancy awoke to the chill of early morning air. The fire had dwindled to glowing embers. Sara had not moved; her face still revealed the pacific beauty of sleeping innocence. David's arm had grown heavy across her stomach, and she reached for his hand to move his arm to her hip. The hand she touched was cold and stiff; the arm had the heaviness of a log.

Nancy threw off the quilt and whirled toward her sleeping husband. His body rolled face down in the dirt toward the dying fire. Nancy's howl resounded through the encampment; the wailing of her grief chased her husband's spirit to the skies.

The softness of the young child, Sara, wrapped around Nancy's shoulders and rocked with her in rhythm to the groaning of her soul.

* * * * * * * * * *

On the slope above the stockade, Nancy stood opposite the preacher and watched as the soldiers dug a shallow grave. She wondered how many others would lie with David in this place of interment before the removal was complete. David's life was lost in battle, no matter how personal or futile it might have been; he died with the heart of the warrior. The others would succumb to the hunger, filth, and eviscerating misery of the defeated.

David lay at her feet, his face covered with a handkerchief from Nancy's purse. The medical officer spoke to brother Samuels and placed something in his hand.

The soldiers averted their eyes as they placed David in the freshly turned soil. Nancy stared at the grove of trees in front of her—one an ancient oak that had towered over humanity for many lifetimes. Hunters had hidden themselves among its boughs, and children had swung from its lower limbs; it had sheltered man and beast beneath its open arms for two hundred years. Somber, dignified, it now stood in the stillness of the moment and presided over the return of David to the elements of his origin. Through the lush foliage of its branches, the morning sun, still low in the eastern sky, thrust shafts of light over David's grave. It warmed the lids of Nancy's eyes, as she looked down and saw all that remained on the grass was a ragged mound of clods and soil.

Nodding to brother Samuels and signaling a guard to remain, the medical officer gave the order for the burial detail to return to the stockade.

Nancy and the preacher were motionless, fixed in silence, interrupted by brother Samuels' quivering, anguished sigh. Nancy saw him raise his eyes to heaven in supplication. She knew he had prayed and pled and worked on behalf of the Cherokees. Now, he stayed to offer what he could—support, comfort—perhaps, the right words—which eluded him, because nothing was right anymore.

Steeling himself to verbalize the thoughts of his heart, brother Samuels invoked the Almighty: "May the soul of David Hilderbrand find rest in the realm of Paradise." He choked, "And may his wife and child have Thy divine protection and care as they walk the path of this life with courage and with faith."

Nancy wanted to feel bitter toward this man, whose God had forsaken them, whose people had herded and corralled them like cattle. But she sensed his genuine concern and frustration. He had taught them to look for blessing in adversity, to grow stronger in hardship, to wait patiently on the Lord. She wondered if he was having difficulty applying his own lessons. He, at least, could work out his salvation in a home of his own choosing.

Hat in hand, penitent of the sins of his people, brother Samuels stood before her. "Mrs. Hilderbrand, I am very sorry about your husband. He was a good man—one of the brightest students at the mission school."

Nancy did not speak.

"The medical officer said to give this to you." He handed Nancy the gold wedding band David had worn on a thong around his neck. Nancy's tears were salty as they seeped in the corners of her mouth. A sob caught his breath. "It should not have been." Turning away, he pulled his hat down on his head. "This whole affair should not be!"

As she preceded the guard back to the stockade, Nancy lowered the shawl from her head and tugged it across her shoulders, wrapping her arms within it and around her body, like a creature

17

forming a chrysalis. But the only metamorphosis occurring was in the unborn child; Nancy was simply the cocoon, an insensate protective shell.

Nancy stood at the cinders of their campfire and looked at the place where they had lain. Sara had folded the baby's blanket and the cover Nancy had shared with David; she had arranged them beside the tree trunk with the few remaining possessions. Yesterday was so far away, she thought. Yesterday, she had David, she had a home, and she had a hope that precluded fear. How swift and heavy were the feet of misfortune!

Nancy tied the leather around her neck and tucked David's ring behind her collar, dropping it down her bodice. She realized she was weak and shivering. As soon as she sank to the ground, Sara appeared with a hefty box she placed at Nancy's feet. Sara scurried to unfold the quilt and threw it around Nancy's back, lapping it over and tucking it, as if she were bundling a baby. Nancy noticed in the box an allotment of rations—corn meal, salt pork, coffee, a frying pan, brewing pot, tin mugs and utensils. Nancy asked, "Can you make coffee?"

The child nodded in response. "I made coffee for my father."

Nancy asked, "Would you make some for me, please?"

The child seemed eager to help and started to fetch water. She stopped. "What do I call you?"

Nancy looked at the child for a long, still moment. "My name is Nancy—Nancy Hilderbrand."

* * * * * * * * *

Sara had made fire and brewed coffee. In the warmth of late May, the Month of the Planting Moon, Nancy remained wrapped against the chill winds threatening to topple her. She held the tin mug with both hands and willed the heat to warm her.

"Nancy Hilderbrand."

Nancy raised her head toward the Cherokee voice.

"We are family," said the woman. "I am Kaquoli Hicks of Running Water Town. I am your husband's cousin. I have brought you some food." She offered Nancy some cornbread, wrapped in newspaper.

Nancy shook her head. "I am not hungry."

"You must eat," Kaquoli insisted. "The girl, Sara, looked for your people. She said you are with child. You must eat for the child."

"The child has no father. He is dead."

"But you are not dead. Your grief will not kill you, but it can kill the child. Your husband trusts you to care for his child." Kaquoli thrusted the food toward Nancy. "Eat."

Nancy took the bread and bowed her head. "Please, sit, Kaquoli."

The woman tucked her skirt beneath her and lowered herself to the ground. She was nearly thirty, Nancy surmised—tall, sturdy, handsome. Streaks of silver in her black braid glistened in the sunlight, and her green eyes, the color of the springtime forest, betrayed her mixed parentage.

19

Nancy ate as Kaquoli watched. Sara brought more coffee for Nancy and a cup for Kaquoli.

"She is a good daughter." Kaquoli said of Sara. "But she is not yours."

"No," replied Nancy. "Her mother is dead, and she was separated from her father." They watched as Sara stirred the coals to extinguish the fire and prepared to take the utensils for washing.

"We are both alone now," said Nancy.

"Not alone," said Kaquoli. "You have your child."

Nancy studied the grease spots on the empty fold of newsprint in her hand. "Yes, the child," she sighed.

"I am alone, also," said Kaquoli. There was a fullness of silence. "I loved once," she continued, "but never married." She took the paper from Nancy's hand and twisted it before throwing it in the fire pit. "A white trader. He went away—never came back."

Nancy asked, "You have other family?"

"A sister—married to a white. They own a farm on the river near Shake Rag. You?"

"Two older brothers. When I married, they were in New Echota. I don't know where they are now—maybe dead."

Sara returned with a bucket of water. Taking their cups, she ladled water into them, rinsed them, tossed the contents on the grass, and upended the cups on the tree trunk to drain.

Nancy called, "Come, Sara—sit."

The girl sat at Nancy's feet. She took Sara's hand and pressed it between her own.

"Thank you, Sara Colaquee. You have been a helper and a friend to me. Stay with me until you find your father. We will be family."

Sara smiled and nodded.

Kaquoli said, "Nancy, you and Sara join me at my campfire. I have made preparations for leaving since the Cold Moon. I did not want to go, but I believed the time would come. I have food and blankets to share. I have extra clothes for you, but none for Sara." Kaquoli looked at the ground before her. "I do not want to be alone."

Nancy looked at Sara, then replied, "We will join you at your fire. And I have my sewing supplies. If I have material, I can make whatever Sara needs."

Kaquoli stood and nodded. "Good." She motioned to Sara. "Put the coffee pot and mugs in the rations box, and I will carry it for you." Sara complied and handed the box to Kaquoli, who directed, "You stay to help Nancy. You know the place of my camp." Tossing her heavy braid over her shoulder, Kaquoli padded away.

Nancy rose to her feet. "Sara, go with Kaquoli," she insisted. "There is little to carry. I will find you."

Sara hesitated but went as she was told.

Nancy watched the girl's departure and saw her turn to look back. Nancy nodded, urging her to go on. Sara disappeared around the corner of the stable.

Nancy surveyed the place of her last contentment. Lying in the shelter of David's body, his arm caressing their unborn child,

Nancy had lost her fear in the awareness of his love and in the hypnotic blaze of the fire. She picked up the stick with which Sara had stirred the embers—now nothing but ashes.

Nancy retrieved the quilt that had fallen from her shoulders. She hugged it to her body, burying her face in the smell of the earth, of the smoke, of David.

Nancy picked up the baby blanket Sara had laid on top of Nancy's purse beside the sewing basket. She noticed the soft wool was smudged with blood from David's wound. "This is all that remains of your father," she must tell the child. "A soldier struck him when he attacked the blue coat captain. This is true. But, even before your birth, your father loved you and tried to defend you from those who would take your home, your land, your heritage."

Nancy turned, leaving the remnants of the encampment behind her. She set out to find the fire ring of Kaquoli.

* * * * * * * * *

A month had passed, and the heat of summer was upon them, suffocating their days and bringing to their nights the sounds of the sickly season—coughs, the moans of dysentery, the cries of sleepless, feverish children—an occasional death wail. David no longer rested alone on the hillside.

The river, dark and deceptively sluggish, flowed at the foot of the hill upon which squatted the picketed stockade. During the summer months, mosquitoes bred along its banks, thriving on the

22

blood of man and beast, spreading disease and death among the weak and aged. The Cherokee, the Creek, the Chickamauga—they knew the Giver was hungry; his stomach growled in the sickly season. They avoided the Tennessee at this time of year; but the white men herded their people like cattle onto the flatboats, loading the vessels with fresh flesh, forging headlong into the great belly, through the twisting, churning, convoluted intestines of the mighty river.

Kaquoli and Nancy sat before the fire—no longer for warmth, but for relief from the nighttime torment of mosquitoes. Sara lay asleep, her head on Nancy's lap. Nancy felt the child's cheek and brow and stroked her hair, reassuring herself there was no fever.

"You know, the child may not survive if we go overland," declared Kaquoli. "I think they will not take another boat. The Narrows is dangerous any time of year, but in draught! What do these ignorant blue coats know of the river? We should be leading them!"

"Where would you go, Kaquoli? If you could get out, where would you go? You have no home, no land. What would you do?"

Kaquoli stared into the fire. "I would go to the home of my sister. They own much land, and I am strong. I am a good worker. They would welcome me there."

Nancy threw more sticks into the fire. "I have no place. My parents are dead. Another lives on my father's land. My brothers may already be in the West."

"You would come with me," Kaquoli affirmed.

Nancy smiled. "You are generous with the land of your brother-in-law."

"It is the land of my sister, too," she declared. Then, nodding, she admitted, "But my brother-in-law is a good man, kind, generous. He would welcome the three of us."

Lingering in the silence of thought, Nancy's delicate fingers removed the strands of hair sticking to Sara's face and combed them with her fingertips back into the loose braid puddled in Nancy's lap. "The child will not die. We will escape."

"How? You see the guards, the pickets. There is no way but the gate." Kaquoli waited for a response. "And we are many miles from my sister's farm."

Nancy raised her hand. "I must think."

Kaquoli shook her head, leaving Nancy with her thoughts.

Nancy broke the long silence. "When the gambling boat comes, the soldiers leave with the women who will dance and drink."

Kaquoli retorted, "I do not dance and drink. Do you now dance and drink?"

Nancy smiled. "It is an opportunity to make our way out."

Again, Kaquoli shook her head. "And what about the child? Eight years old and straight as a stick—will the soldiers take her to dance and drink?"

Nancy frowned. After a few moments, she muttered, "Burnett."

"What?" asked Kaquoli.

"I will tell you when it is time, Kaquoli. Prepare carefully, as you did for the removal. But this time, take only what you can carry in your handbag."

* * * * * * * * *

As she searched among the cabins and stables, Nancy noted the encampments were reduced to a third. How many of those who had left for the Promised Land, she wondered, would arrive to see if it flowed with streams as pure, through forests as lush, over land as rich as that which had been theirs?

Nancy had determined to return for breakfast with Kaquoli and Sara, when she saw Private Burnett carrying a saddle out of the stable. Throwing a stirrup strap over the hitching post, he placed the saddle astride the cross rail and prepared to wax and brush the leather seat. Nancy's tread was soft as she approached the private and halted before him.

Burnett looked up in surprise. "Ma'am! How are you?" Stammering, he remembered. "I was awful sorry to hear about your husband."

"Thank you, Mr. Burnett," Nancy replied.

Burnett wiped his brow with the polishing cloth in his hand. Glancing around him, he asked, "Is there anything I can do for you?"

"Perhaps."

"Well, ma'am…"

"My name is Nancy—Nancy Hilderbrand."

"Well, Mrs. Hilderbrand, if you're needing more rations, I can see what I can do. You're with child, I heard. You may be needing more food."

"No, we have enough, thank you. She hesitated. "I want you to help me leave the camp, Private Burnett."

The soldier began waxing the saddle. "I'm sorry, I didn't hear what you said."

"I want you to help my child, my cousin, and me to escape from this stockade."

Ignoring Nancy, Burnett said, "I am not understanding a word of what you are saying. You best be going back to your camp."

"Mr. Burnett, you have a wife. Perhaps you will have a child very soon. You have seen the injustice done to my people. Your men have killed my husband, when he was only protecting me. You saw with your own eyes."

The private was buffing the gleaming leather. Nancy knew he was listening.

"I want my baby to be born in the land of his people. I have another child who looks to me as her mother. I do not want the girl to die. My cousin is my only family. We are three women with no land, no weapons. We do not fight against you. We have never done you any harm."

Private Burnett looked up from his work and over Nancy's shoulder. He glanced into her eyes. "Nancy, you go eat your breakfast. I'll come 'round to see you later in the day." Nodding his head, he announced, "Good morning, Sarge. You get your saddle; I'll polish it up for you."

"Thanks, Burnett," the passing soldier said in response, as he perused Nancy and winked at the private.

Nancy avoided the eyes of the sergeant and returned the way she had come.

* * * * * * * * *

Nancy sat with her purse in her lap and the sewing basket at her side. Again, she must determine the essential value of her meager possessions. Opening the drawstrings of the bag, she removed the etui and noted that it held a few needles and a thimble. She dropped the case back in the purse. She left David's tobacco pouch in the basket but removed his pipe. The sweet, smoky smell of the bowl reminded her of peaceful times by their hearth. Their stomachs filled with the bounty from their garden and orchard, they would sit; she would sew, David would read, sometimes they would doze together. Nancy put the pipe in her handbag. She returned the remaining two handkerchiefs and pulled the drawstrings.

"What did you have in mind?" The voice at her back startled her.

She looked up into the face of Private Burnett.

He fidgeted as he scanned the area around them and spoke in a subdued voice. "I can't fight my conscience. My wife would have me to free all of you, if I could. At least I can do something."

"At the time of the next gambling boat, when the men take some of our women to the river, come get us. Just get us outside the gate with the rest. You can come back—say you changed your mind—say you did not want to betray your wife."

"But the child—how do we get her out?"

"She can wait near the gate till the men and women return. They will be noisy and drunk. She can slip out around them while the gate is open."

"Be ready," he commanded, then sauntered away.

* * * * * * * * *

It was only two nights before Burnett appeared at their fire. "You girls ready for a bit of fun?"

"Hey, Burnie, we'll wait for you at the dock!" cried one of the blue coats on his way to the gate. His voice sounded above the raucous throng of soldiers and giggling women, who were so eager to sell their souls for a few hours of freedom.

Nancy and Kaquoli exchanged glances. Then Nancy looked at Sara and ached with love and concern. The girl knew what she must do, but could an eight-year old child find the energy to stay awake and the perception and courage to flee at the opportune time?

Sara ran to Nancy and hugged her around her skirt.

Nancy smoothed Sara's hair. "We will see you in a few hours. Do as I said, and don't be afraid." Taking the leather strip from around her neck, Nancy tied the thong holding David's ring and placed it over Sara's head. "You may borrow this. It will help you to be strong and brave. You must bring it to me at the oak tree."

"Come on, girls. Let's get going!" Burnett encouraged.

Kaquoli and Nancy picked up their handbags, joined Burnett, and followed the revelers. Passing through the gate, Nancy noticed the guards, who were smoking their pipes with their rifles at their sides, lazily propped against the outer pickets.

They had walked fifty yards or more into an area of shadows, when Burnett said, "You girls go on with the others." He jerked his head toward the density of the nearby trees. "I'm not feeling too good. I need to go back for a bit." He started back, then turned and shouted into the emptiness, "No, now you go on. I'll see if I don't get to feeling better soon."

From their concealment, Nancy and Kaquoli could see the guards, could see them stand to confront Burnett. "Hey, soldier, where you going? Thought you were headed off to the landing."

Burnett did not respond.

"I asked you a question, Private," the sergeant demanded.

They could not see Burnett's face, but they heard him stammer, "I-I-I just couldn't do it, sir." He hung his head.

"Couldn't do what, soldier?"

Burnett hesitated, his nervousness only making him more credible. "Well, I just been married a year. My wife's the sweetest woman in the world. I just couldn't go carry on like that with the others."

The guards roared in laughter at his expense, and one slapped Burnett on the back. "What a waste of good-looking squaws!"

Burnett acted embarrassed. "I told the girls to go on with the others. They think I got sick, but I just couldn't do it. Excuse me, I'm going to the bunkhouse." He went slinking through the gate like a whipped dog.

Nancy and Kaquoli slipped from their hiding place and made their way toward the graveyard, to the aegis of the trunk of the ancient oak. There, Nancy would wait near David with his kinswoman. They would pray for the young girl Sara to come to them.

* * * * * * * * *

In a few hours, dawn would be lighting the sky. The rousing music wafting back from the river had died; and the boisterous, dissonant chorus of voices began trickling up the rise. Insisting Kaquoli wait by the oak, Nancy crept closer where she might view the gate. The guards were sitting at a makeshift table to one side. Their game interrupted, they began picking up cards, as the revelers approached as coveys of women and blue uniforms—laughing, staggering, groping, some stopping for a final drink and smashing a bottle to climax their celebration. Nancy watched the women and felt ashamed.

Where was the child? Had she fallen asleep? There had been opportunities—when the guards were encircled by their comrades, who made crude remarks about the high times forfeited to their stay of duty; the commotion when one drunk began swinging at another and the guards had to intervene and drag them both inside the stockade. Nancy could see no more figures funneling into the compound. The guards prepared to close the gate and to move their vigil inside to the portholes cut between the pickets.

Nancy was seized with a desire to run to the gates to demand reentry. Sara was alone. She must get to the child! Trying to steel her will and compose her thoughts, she knew she must tell Kaquoli to go alone. Whatever befell them on the long trail to the West, Nancy must be with Sara. Perhaps she was not thinking of the child to come, but Sara was here and now. The thought of her facing the perils of the trek—perhaps, even death, with no one to hold her hand or cool her fevered brow—was more than Nancy could bear. She would return.

Nancy, with the instinct of a creature of the night forest, crept up the slope, around the rude grave markers, to the trunk of the oak tree. Kaquoli moved from her seat among the roots to a crouching position, as if she were ready to pounce or to dart. Nancy shook her head. "I did not see the child. I am going back. You go on without us."

"I will not go," stated Kaquoli.

"You must. Go! Go to your sister's farm and start a new life. Plant your feet in the soil of our people and do not be moved."

Tears glistened in Kaquoli's eyes, as she took Nancy's hand and whispered, "God be with you, my sister."

"My heart will be with you, Kaquoli," Nancy responded, before turning to race back to camp.

A movement in the foliage to their right caused the women to shrink back in the shadows against the tree. Their breathing shallow, their hearts throbbing, they waited and prayed the soldiers were not patrolling the perimeter of the grounds.

"Nancy—Kaquoli," came the furtive voice of the child.

"Sara?" Nancy crept toward the sound.

Hair disheveled but smiling, Sara came out of the bushes, carrying the sewing basket with one hand and dragging behind her the quilt, stuffed and tied.

Nancy gathered the girl in her arms, as Kaquoli relieved her of her burdens.

"Oh, Sara! What kept you? And what is all this? I told you to leave the rest—just get yourself out."

Kaquoli placed the basket and bag next to the tree trunk, knelt beside Sara, and placed her arms around the child. Sara put her arm around Kaquoli's neck.

"I didn't want you to leave your sewing basket. And Kaquoli had left the clothes and the coffee—the other things. We need these for our journey. I brought them."

Nancy smiled and Kaquoli rolled her eyes toward heaven.

Nancy asked, "How did you get out with all of it? I didn't see you leave the stockade."

"The guards are very lazy. They were drinking. I watched from inside the gate. One guard went to the outhouse, and the other was drinking and playing with the cards with his back turned. I was able to go and return, and he didn't even see me."

"You came out more than once?" Kaquoli asked in surprise.

Sara nodded. "First to bring the quilt. I left it around the corner of the stockade. I waited until I heard the voices coming from the river, and, when the guards were busy with the drunken soldiers, I moved behind the crowd, the skirts of the women. I am small and your basket was not heavy—I moved very fast." Sara removed the ring from her neck and returned it to Nancy. "I was not afraid. Now, you must have courage."

"We all must." Retying the leather around her neck, Nancy said, "We will find a place to rest and then begin tomorrow. We have a long way to go." The women continued up the hill behind the fort, into the cool depths of the forest.

* * * * * * * * *

The undulating ridges rippled away to the west—the river twisting and writhing like a giant serpent at their feet. The women were in the elements of their origin. Nancy recalled the scripture that encouraged faithful endurance in the trial of life: "Since we are surrounded by such a great a cloud of witnesses, let us run with patience." They now walked among a cloud of witnesses, who wept over the bondage of the Aniyunwiya—the Real People, but among whom David's spirit soared and rejoiced over the freedom of his wife, this child, and his kinswoman. His own child would be born in the valley his people had trod for a thousand years, on the banks of the mighty, tumultuous river—the Cherokee's River, the old ones' giver of life.

Nancy knew there would be a hole in her heart till the end of her days, but she could patch it with memory and darn it with the love and labor required of a mother. She had a strong back, tireless hands, and the task of caring for the children. Challenge, satisfaction, and contentment would sustain her until her spirit might join David's in the chorus of voices singing through the winds of the valley, in the gurgling of the streams slashing through the ridges, and in the rustling branches of the forest.

In the shadows of the mountains at their shoulders to the north and at their backs to the east, the women trudged westward, tracing the river wending its way through the valley. Silent and steady, they walked through the day, foraging for food along the way. At night, they made camp and rested in the shelter of the overhanging limestone cliffs, or in caves darkened by the soot of generations of fires, around which hunters had regaled themselves with tales of conquest, or healers had sought the curative power of prayers rising with smoke to the heart of the mountain mother.

Their last day on the trail, Nancy awoke with the sun flaming above the mountains to the east, the clouds puffing and swirling like smoke rising from the burning peaks. Nancy slipped from the quilt she shared with the child and crept out from their rock shelter to the ridge overlooking the valley. From the precipice, she basked in the glory of the morning and rejoiced in the hope of the new day.

Seizing deep breaths of cool, sweet air, Nancy filled her lungs and cleared her mind. Driven by fear and the instinct for survival for so many weeks, Nancy now had the luxury of time to set in order the confused storeroom of her soul. She must find a place in her heart to hope and plan for the future; another to organize and store the memories of the past; and, still, another to conquer and control the demons of anger and hatred. Every thought of David scratched a tender wound, but she sensed healing was taking place. One day there would be a scar—an indelible remembrance of injury, yet callused and without pain.

Nancy looked down through the trees to the river coursing through the depression between the ridges. In its fertile alluvial soil, her people had staked their settlements and planted their staple crops since time began. With the mountains' huddling them like a mother hen, they found sustenance from the river, the earth, the forest—and, when necessary, found refuge under the mother's wing by fleeing and disappearing into her bosom.

As Nancy's soul found peace with the dawning of the new day, her ears caught the faint sound of riders, the creaking of wagon wheels, voices snapping indecipherable commands. The wail of a baby rose above muted coughs along with the frantic yap of a tethered dog.

"What do you see?" whispered Kaquoli, slipping next to Nancy on the projection overlooking the slope.

Crawling to the cover of a pine branch, Nancy gestured to Kaquoli to follow.

From their concealment, they waited and watched as the sounds came closer.

"Nancy? Kaquoli? Where are you?" Shielding sleepy eyes from the light, Sara emerged from her pallet under the ledge.

Scurrying to the child, Nancy wrapped her arm around her, covered Sara's mouth with her hand, and pulled her back to the refuge of the evergreens. "Quiet!" Nancy blew into Sara's ear.

From their place on the overhang, the women watched as a convoy of people, wagons, and horses approached on the old warpath, now the over-mountain trail, twisting toward the west through the trees below. The moving scene flickered through the foliage: mounted bluecoats escorting a massive assemblage of people—on foot, on horse or mule back, in ox carts, in carriages, prodding livestock, dragging sleds loaded with possessions, supplies—the sick, the aged. Mothers, expressionless save for deep creases between their brows, with children in tow and in pouches at their breasts. One shifted the toddler sleeping on her shoulder to ease the pain in her weary back. A warrior, bent in defeat, his right arm in a sling, his eye blackened and swollen, glanced up toward the canopy of evergreens. Nancy sensed he felt their presence, but he returned his gaze to the forest floor.

Cherokee, mixed bloods, some blacks. Some rich, some poor. Old men and women withered and broken. Young men who had burned in their anger beyond feeling. The dying, the dead. Faces blank or etched with fear, misery, bewilderment, only a few still alive with hatred and the lust for revenge. A panorama of civilized humanity in the throes of uncivilized treatment.

Having deceived the course of destiny, the women watched and wept from their aerie on the mount.

* * * * * * * * *

Sara searched the faces she spied through the trees, but none was the visage of her father. She had carried the memory with her— her father, tall and strong, pulling her braid; saying, as usual, "Good coffee"; taking his rifle and ax and heading into the forest.   He had raised his rifle in salute before leaving the clearing, where their cabin was rising, room by room, a quarter mile from their nearest neighbor.

Sara had rinsed the dishes and was feeding scraps to the hog penned beside the shed at the rear of the cabin, when she heard the horses' approaching. Coming around the side of the log structure and seeing the blue uniforms, she dropped the slop pot and raced across the clearing to follow her father. But, before she could enter the woods, she was seized around the waist and snatched up by a mounted soldier, who held her, drooping at his side like a sack of meal.

Kicking and clawing the arm binding her, Sara refused to answer their questions of "Where are you parents? Are there others beside you? What is your name?" She willed her father to come to her, to know she needed him.

"Put her on the wagon with the others," said the leader with the plumed hat. "We'll have Hawes check back, see if her parents have returned, and pick them up with their belongings."

The soldier prodded his horse to lope out to the dray, waiting where the trail entered the clearing. He placed Sara on her knees at the edge of the open wagon, in the center of which a young mother, dark braid flowing over her shoulder, sat on a crate to suckle her baby. Their feet dangling like rag dolls, four others sat around the perimeter of the bed. There was an old man, his head turbaned, his coal eyes glinting within a withered, brown, walnut face, and an old woman, perhaps his wife, curled like a gray opossum within the shawl pulled across her shoulders and wrapped around the fists in her lap. A young lion of a man, chest and shoulders broad, muscles stretching the deerskin taut on his upper arms, chiseled face twitching with anger at the jaw line, cast murderous glances at his captors, as he twisted his hands that were bound with rope at his back. And a boy, about twelve or thirteen, dressed only in overalls and barefooted—a reedy stripling—rubbed tears from his eyes and wiped his nose on the bib of his trousers.

Sara sat and turned to peer into the forest. Her father would come at any moment to rescue her. His rifle would fire, and, like crows feeding in the corn, the soldiers would scatter before his war cries.

"Hey, up!" shouted the captain in the broad brim, as he reined his horse alongside the wagon. The dray jerked and creaked as the team of horses made the tight turn back on the trail. "Move on east along the river, Corporal!" he commanded. Sara could hear the squeaking leather of his saddle and tall boots, as he spurred his mount to the lead position. The cart bumped eastward. Sara bent her knees and wrapped her arms around her legs, pulling them to her chest. Against the material covering her knees, she pressed her eyelids to contain her tears.

Her fathers was the first face Sara could remember. Often, her fear of being alone in the dark had faded with the irresistible sleep of the weary child, but the face of her father would greet her with the morning light. He always came back with his funny stories and games, teasing and tickling. Once he brought her a flute he had whittled, once a golden eagle feather. He rarely hugged and only a few times had struck her—when she misbehaved or was too slow— but she knew he loved her. She was not cold or hungry or frightened in the light of day, until the day her father went into the woods and the soldiers came. Though she did not fully comprehend the meaning of the passing processional, Sara now believed she would never see her father's face again.

The last of the guards passed from sight, and the trail was again silent. Only the muffled sobs of Sara, as she wept into Nancy's bosom, disrupted the stillness of the moment.

Kaquoli whispered, "Now we are safe. Let us go. We are only a few hours from Shake Rag."

They folded their pallets, gathered their possessions, and followed their brethren into the way of the sun.

* * * * * * * * *

The women rested in the heat of the day on the ridge above Shake Rag, nestled in the curve of the valley. In the distance below, clearings in the trees marked the settlement of the riverside community, where the saw mill and an incipient coal mining enterprise had necessitated a river landing and supply store.

Kaquoli made idle tracings in the dirt with a hickory twig, while Sara napped in Nancy's lap. "There, just to the east, is the farm of my brother-in-law." Kaquoli pointed with the stick to the area where the river began to coil back upon itself. "He owns the grist mill and saw mill. He came as a trader into the area several years ago and met my sister. Our father had many acres on both sides of the river, from Running Water Town to the Suck. He would have given a piece of land to Silas, but Silas said, 'No, I will buy it from you.' Silas registered the deed. It was all done according to the new law."

"Silas was a wise man," Nancy remarked, as she stroked Sara's loose hair flowing over her lap.

"Yes, so it seems," agreed Kaquoli with a sigh, digging a hole with the end of the stick. "When my father was dying, Silas sat with him and held my father's hand. They loved and trusted each other—like father and son." She brushed her cheek with the back of her hand.

"When did you leave your father's home?" Nancy asked.

"I remained until Silas and Peggy—my sister's English name—were married and had settled into the cabin Silas had built on his land. I left a few days later to go upriver to Stanley, to the home of my aunt. My uncle had died not long before my father. I helped my aunt with the farm and with the mission school." Kaquoli explained, "She and my mother were English Cherokee. Their mother was a white missionary schoolteacher, who gave up her people for the love of my grandfather—the brother of David's grandfather. When my aunt died, I stayed on the farm and kept the mission school going. Until the removal, of course." Kaquoli tapped three small stones into the hole.

"How long has it been since you have seen your sister, Kaquoli?" Nancy probed.

"I have seen her only once since the wedding—when my aunt died." Kaquoli knew Nancy was watching, and she avoided her gaze. She sighed, "Six, seven years—a long time. I have not even seen my nephew since he was a baby." She threw the stick down through the trees. "Peggy and I are of different minds. I have held to the ways of the old ones." Kaquoli shook her head and exhaled, "It seems, perhaps, Peggy was right—the future is in the hands of the white man."

The silence pressed upon them like a fog. Kaquoli watched Nancy as she coiled the length of Sara's hair.

"No, I think, not Kaquoli. The future is in our own hands. We must make a way for ourselves. Whether it be white, Cherokee, or something in between—it must be a way that is right and good for us." Nancy sighed, "And I must make a way for the children."

Kaquoli longed for Nancy's courage and determination. Like the evergreen growing from the mountain cliffs, gusts might bend and twist her, leaving her scarred, but she would survive with deep roots holding fast. Kaquoli thought herself a hardwood—flourishing in the old forest, snapping branches as the breeze brushed limbs together—easily burned. She was a woman of organization, planning, control; she needed certainty, security. She could envision no place for herself, yet, in the uncertain time ahead. The fog dampened her spirits and blurred her vision of the future.

* * * * * * * * *

Their path led them between the landing store and the shed that served as the coal mining office, then eastward on the river road curving through Shake Rag.

In the middle of the afternoon, only a few people were milling about, and they passed with little notice, though greeted into the settlement by yapping dogs, circling their feet and stirring up dust in excitement.

"Carol…Kaquoli?"

42

The women, startled, turned toward the deep rumble of a man's voice. A giant, auburn-haired bear of a man had been loading supplies into the bed of his wagon. Holding a fifty-pound sack of feed as if it were a feather pillow, he had halted in surprise at the sight of the women and child.

Kaquoli hesitated, then responded, "Silas."

Tossing the sack on the wagon, the man came to Kaquoli, with his hands extended to take hers. The faint melody of his native tongue tinted his words with golden warmth. "Oh, Kaquoli, it's so good to see you! We've been so worried!"

Kaquoli smiled and lowered her head. "I am well, Silas, as you can see." Gesturing toward her comrades, Kaquoli said, "This is Nancy Hilderbrand, my friend, and her adopted daughter, Sara Colaquee. Nancy, Sara, this is my sister's husband, Silas McKinnon." Silas tipped his hat to them.

Silas continued, "We had heard you had been taken with the Cherokee up river."

"We were taken," Kaquoli answered, with a nod toward Nancy and Sara. She smiled. "But my clever friend here devised a plan for our escape from Ross's Landing."

Silas squeezed her hands and shook her arms emphatically. "Why didn't you come to us before? You would have been safe with us. We have heard many are dying on the way to the West."

"I wanted to go with our people," Kaquoli explained, "but then I realized this is where I belong—with my family, in the land of our people."

Silas pressed Kaquoli's hands together in his engulfing grip and placed his forehead against them. "Thanks be to God you're all right!"

Kaquoli saw a flicker of question in Nancy's eyes, freed her hands, and said, "Silas, we are fine. Do you think you and Peggy might find a space for us to stay for a while—until we can get our own place?"

"No doubt about it! Here, let me take your things." Silas loaded their possessions on the back of his wagon. "Miss Sara," he smiled, "mind if I set you right here on top of this feed sack?"

Sara shook her head, and Silas swung the child up onto the wagon. "Now, you hold to the side and don't stand up till we get to the house." Silas glanced at Nancy's expanding waistline and at the ring on her hand. "Mrs. Hilderbrand, you and Carol— excuse me, Kaquoli—"

"No, Silas," interrupted Kaquoli, "'Carol' will be fine."

"And call me 'Nancy,'" Nancy corrected. "I am a widow."

Silas looked down at the ground and sighed, "I'm sorry." Clearing his throat, he continued, "Well, Nancy, you and Carol ride up front with me." He helped the women to the buckboard, then circled the wagon to take his seat and the reins. "This will be quite a surprise for Peggy and Josiah. He's grown since you last saw him, Carol—a fine, strong, handsome boy." He released the brake; and, with the slap of leather across their backs, the horses took the trail toward home.

The trees formed a canopy overhead as they proceeded along the river trail. Flickers of light filtering through the leaves, fluttering across Carol's face as she looked up at the faraway ceiling of blue. She felt safe, but an uneasy doubt gnawed a far corner of her mind.

A couple of miles eastward, a stacked stone fence from the trail to the river marked the beginning of the McKinnon property. Trailside, the farm was edged by split rails, along which grew heavy honeysuckle vines, their fragrance strong and sweet in the remaining heat of the day. When only about six or seven, Carol had shown her younger sister how to break the base of a blossom to pull the center from the petals and with it the drop of nectar on the pistil. That single drop brushed on the tongue was sweet, sublime, and precious. They were good times—happy, innocent, and so long ago.

* * * * * * * * *

As she bounced along on the wagon seat, Nancy realized she had gripped the deerskin handbag under her bulging belly until her fists were stiff and sore. Spreading her fingers across the folds of skirt on her knees, she appraised her small, sturdy hands, the backs a tangle of veins and tendons. They were strong hands, capable of much good work—from sewing fine seams to chopping firewood, from picking and preparing herbs for healing potions to skinning and cooking a squirrel or rabbit for stewing. She had money in the bag to buy a piece of ground large enough for a cabin and garden patch; She could make a way for herself and Sara. She hoped she

45

could persuade Kaquoli to stay with her, at least until the child was born and her life was settled.

Nancy glanced aside at her friend—now "Carol," she reminded herself. Carol's thoughts were lost with her gaze somewhere beyond the treetops. She seemed so calm, so stable, and Nancy wished she could find the same serenity. Her mind was churning. She felt driven by the need to work, to give substance to the plans laid out in her head. She needed to prove herself, and she could not fail.

The split rail fencing turned at a wide path toward the McKinnon home, set in a clearing between trail and river. The house was a roomy, two-story frame structure with a single-story addition at one end, and what appeared to be the original log cabin at the other. Nancy's thoughts were echoed by Carol's observation, "You certainly have enlarged your house, Silas."

Silas laughed and replied, "Well, Carol, I'm a big man. I get to feeling cramped from time to time and need a bit more space. Besides, I'm a miller. I like to work with wood. Building gives me great pleasure."

Nancy ventured, "Well, then, perhaps, Mr. McKinnon, you might be available for hire to build a small cabin for me when I find some land?"

Reining his team to a halt before a wide planked porch, Silas responded, "Nancy, I'd consider it an honor and a privilege to help you get settled."

Silas moved to the back of the wagon and swung Sara down with a wide sweep that sent her skirt flying out behind her, bringing the first laugh Nancy had heard from the child. He then moved to help the women to the ground, while adding, "I just might be able to help you find you a good piece of land too, Nancy."

"Thank you, Silas. I would greatly appreciate your help." Nancy felt the first step had been taken, and her footing seemed sure and solid.

The trio followed Silas up the steps to the porch and waited while he removed his boots, set them on the stool by the door, and capped them with his hat.

"Peggy! Peg-gy! Brought you company!" he bellowed through the front door and open window of the log building to their right.

A face flashed at the window seconds before the door was opened and a diminutive likeness of Carol appeared. "Carol! I thought we'd lost you!" Extending her hands, she stepped into her sister's embrace, then stepped back to survey the vision before her. "You're as beautiful as ever. Isn't she, Silas? But you do look a bit tired and worn. Don't you think she looks tired, Silas?" she frowned.

Nancy heard an edge of irritation in Silas's voice, as he responded, "These ladies have walked a long way, Peggy. You'd be tired, too." He gestured toward Nancy. "This is Carol's friend, Mrs. Hilderbrand—Nancy." Standing behind Sara, he tugged at one of the child's braids. "And this young lady's Sara."

47

"Well," Peggy persisted, "don't mind my saying, but you all three look like you need a good feeding and some rest."

"Reckon I could use a good feeding, too." Silas winked at Sara.

Peggy's reply was caustic. "You ain't been in need of a good feeding since you were a baby!"

Nancy was uncomfortable, but she smiled at Sara's giggle and the girl's pleasure at the attention of the amiable Scotsman. Sara's face was alive with the light of childhood for the first time in many weeks. But Carol had said little, and her expression was reserved, if not apprehensive.

They entered a wide hallway leading from front door to back porch of the house, layered within and without with whitewash. To their immediate right, an open doorway led into a dining room edged with a cold fireplace, a black enameled clock stationed on the massive beam mantel. In the center of the room, an oval walnut pedestal table was surrounded by six ladder-back chairs; the one at the head was an arm chair with a loose tapestry cushion in the seat. From the far side of the dining room, the aroma of baking biscuits beckoned from the attached log cabin, now the kitchen, also whitewashed.

To their left, another doorway opened into a parlor with fireplace, now set with logs ready for the first chill of autumn. A well-worn couch and footstool seemed ready to accept Silas's lumbering form. Beyond that, Peggy said, was their bedroom and a smaller room for Josiah.

Straight ahead, a long maple hall bench hugged the wall and terminated at another doorway, leading, Peg said, to stairs ascending to the second story.

Silas interrupted Peggy's tour of the house. "Peg, I told these ladies they could stay with us till they get a place of their own. Think we could settle them in upstairs?"

"I don't see why not. Let's go up and take a look. It's mostly unfinished, but I think we can make do." Peggy took the lead toward the back hallway but turned to snap, "Silas, go ring the bell for Josiah. It's nearly suppertime, and he needs to wash up." Nancy noticed Silas's eyes narrowed and his face flushed as his brawny form moved to comply.

The stairs opened onto an expanse of floored space lighted by three narrow shuttered windows on each side of the house. Mainly used for storage, the room was dry, shaded, and cool, when Peggy opened the shutters and the breeze passed across it. Beside an assemblage of boxes and a camelback trunk, a bare cot rested in one corner. Along rafters opposite it, wire had been stretched from which hung winter coats and clothes, their shoulders covered with cotton sheeting.

"Peggy, this will be very comfortable. Thank you," said Nancy.

"Yes, Peggy, thank you," added Carol. "It has been a long journey. We will sleep well tonight."

"Well, that's just fine," replied Peggy, as she darted about the space, setting out extra blankets and reorganizing as she saw fit.

When she surveyed the area and was satisfied, she ordered, "Now, downstairs. You all can wash up on the back porch, while I see about supper. We'll eat in about twenty minutes."

Nancy noticed dust sparkles floating around Sara as she stood in the light of an open window and rocked a baby's cradle. Seemingly mesmerized by the smooth, gentle swaying caused by the touch of a single finger, Sara's spell was broken by Peggy's explanation. "That was Josiah's. Seems like only yesterday he was in that, and today he's nearly as tall as me." Peggy looked at Sara and quipped, "That's not very tall, is it?"

Sara smiled and said, "It's pretty."

Peggy replied, "Thank you. Silas made it before Josiah was born." Taking Sara's hand and patting it, Peggy said, "He grew so fast, he was hardly in it any time at all. Now, let's go get you something to eat."

Peggy gave them soap, towels, and buckets for washing up and led the way to the back porch to show them the outhouse and spring in the backyard. A boy about Sara's age was dipping water into his mouth and over his head, shaking and slinging his head like a dog, and making his hair stick out in spikes. Sara laughed, and the boy jumped at the sound, then glared at her.

"Nancy, Sara, this is Josiah, our son." Peggy introduced the wet pup, black eyelashes clumping around his deep brown eyes. His face was smooth and tanned, with high cheekbones, but the angle of his nose bespoke the heritage of his English foremother. "He's grown a might since you last saw him, hasn't he, Carol?"

"Josiah, smooth down your hair and come meet these ladies; let your Aunt Carol see you," ordered Peggy. "She hasn't seen you since you were a baby."

Josiah ran his fingers through his hair and wiped his hands on the seat of his overalls. He mounted the steps and halted, slouching, eyes cast down, beside his mother. His head came nearly to her shoulder.

"Josiah's tall like his Pa," said Peggy, "but he's got the look of our father, don't you think, Carol?"

Carol did not respond, but merely extended her hand and said, "I'm happy to see you, Josiah. You're growing into a fine, strong man."

Josiah lifted his eyes to look into those of his aunt and took her hand to shake it. Carol held his gaze and his grip, seeming to will him to stand tall and straight—like a wilted stem rising toward the light. Josiah was perplexed, transfixed, and responded only, "Thank you, ma'am."

Carol, not losing his hand, continued the introductions: "Josiah, these are my friends, Nancy Hilderbrand and Sara Colaquee." Avoiding eye contact with Sara, Josiah nodded toward Nancy.

Peggy stammered, "Well—well, enough. Let's see what I can round up for supper." The door slammed behind her, as she left the women and the boy on the porch.

Nancy and Carol exchanged a brief glance.

"Josiah, please tell your mother Nancy and I are going to walk down where we can see the river before we wash up. We won't be late." Directing her words toward Sara, she ordered, "Sara, go ahead and wash up. Then maybe you and Josiah can play a game of checkers before we eat." Carol noticed the surprise on Josiah's face. "Your father still likes to play checkers, doesn't he?"

Josiah seemed relieved. "Yes, ma'am, he sure does."

Carol smiled and nodded, then motioned for Nancy to follow her.

Sara took a bucket to the spring and filled it halfway. Returning to the porch, she set the bucket on the top step and set herself next to it and lathered a washcloth to wash her face and hands. Then, she rinsed with fresh water, scooping it up in her hands and splashing it against her face. It was good to feel clean and fresh.

"Here's your towel." Her eyes were closed against the water, as Josiah whipped the rough cloth against her head.

Sara dried her face with the towel but held it against her eyes, so the boy could not see her cry.

After several seconds, he asked, "Are you crying?"

Sara did not respond.

"Hey, are you crying?" Josiah jerked the towel away to reveal Sara's tears.

"I didn't mean to make you cry! You made me mad when you laughed at me," he explained.

"You looked funny. Your hair was all stuck out on your head—like this." Sara pulled her braids straight up.

Josiah laughed. "You mean, like this?" He pulled his wet hair into spikes again, and the children giggled as they made silly faces at each other. "Want to play checkers?" Josiah asked.

"I don't know how," responded Sara."

"Come on, I can teach you. My Pa taught me. I can teach you." Sara followed the boy into the parlor, where the game board was setting on a stool in front of the fireplace.

* * * * * * * * *

The river was wide and quiet where it touched the McKinnon property. In the late afternoon breeze, the leaves rustled in the trees, and the gentle lapping and gurgling of water against the boulders along the bank soothed the senses.

"Are you tired, Kaquoli?" asked Nancy.

"No more so than you," Carol smiled in return. "And you better call me 'Carol,' too."

"I will have to remind myself." Nancy breathed a deep sigh as she hugged her arms to herself. "The day the soldiers came, I was standing on our land in a place much like this. It was such a beautiful day, and I was so happy. How could everything change so quickly?"

Carol replied, "Life is like that sometimes. Everything seems so perfect, so settled. Then, in a matter of moments, nothing makes sense anymore." Carol's eyes were filling with tears, and she could not stop their gentle, silent flow.

Her friend moved to stand next to her and asked, "Carol, what is troubling you? You have been uneasy since we neared this place. Can you tell me?"

Carol gathered her thoughts and her composure. She directed her words to the river: "I told you I loved once, and he went away. That was not true. I loved once, and I went away. It was Silas." Carol looked at Nancy and waited for her response.

Nancy's expression bore no judgment, only anticipation: "Silas?"

Carol nodded. "I loved him and thought he loved me. We laughed and talked about everything—even argued about some things, sometimes late into the night. He was a man of intelligence and deep convictions. A good man, a caring man." Carol shook her head and looked at Nancy. "But, nevertheless, a man. I could not compete with Peggy—pretty Peggy, delicate, sweet," she sighed. "I never even tried. I simply backed away and later left."

"Did Silas ever know how you felt?"

"I don't think so, but I think Peggy did. Peggy always got what she wanted, and usually she wanted whatever was mine—or what she thought I wanted."

"She seemed to be genuinely happy to see you today," Nancy observed.

"Perhaps, but she acts as a sister should in such a situation." Carol noticed Nancy's reserve. "You must think me unappreciative.

Just remember, Peggy will always be the hub around which every spoke revolves." Carol turned toward the house. "We'd better get back."

Nancy grasped Carol's arm. "Carol, why did you come back? Knowing all this, why?"

Carol was long in responding as she weighed her words. "The time alone after my aunt died, and the weeks in the stockade, I thought about many things. These people are my family. Love is not always something to be received, but it is always something to be given. I should be near to help as I can." Carol knew Nancy might not understand, but she continued, "Most of all, I came for the sake of the boy. He is still young. When he is older, and his mother is no longer the center of his world, she may be a dark hole that will threaten to swallow him."

"What about Silas? Do you still have feelings for Silas?" asked Nancy.

"I have memories but no more, I think." Carol was unsure as she admitted, "I don't know. Perhaps, while we are here, I will learn what I need to know about myself."

"I hope you are not hurt again," said Nancy.

"No, hurt like that was a thing of youth. I am older and stronger. I know I can make my own way and help the ones I love as I can. That will give me satisfaction."

"When we leave here, will you stay with me for a while, Carol? I have enough to buy a bit of land, and Silas has said he will help me with a house. Will you stay with me, at least until after the baby is born? You may stay with me as long as you want, but, please, stay with me at least that long. I need your help."

* * * * * * * *

As they had hidden behind the tree overlooking the stockade, Carol had seen fear in Nancy's eyes—not for herself, but for the child, alone, frightened. Now, in the eyes of her friend, Carol saw a new fear—that of being alone, of being insufficient to carry the load as she forged into the uncertain future. Carol's direction in life was a careful, plodding, day by day itinerary, in which she tended the necessary, tackled the unexpected, and dreamed of what might have been. Nancy was swift and racing toward goals, but she needed help to relieve the weight against which her feet were struggling.

"Nancy, you have been more of a sister to me in this small time than Peggy ever was. Yes, I will stay and help you." A thought came to Carol: "You will need a teacher for Sara, and for your child, before you know it. Perhaps, I could start a school at Shake Rag. We'd have at least two students right away— Sara and Josiah."

"Let's talk to Silas about it," Nancy suggested. "I'd also like to see how much business there would be for me as a seamstress. I'm sure Silas and Peggy can give us advice."

Carol raised her hand to stop Nancy. "Before we go back, Nancy. Please know, I love my sister, and I know Silas loves her. I would never do anything to come between them. But Peggy is not like other people. She will hurt even those who love her, because no one can love her as much as she loves herself. Now, I will say no more about it." Carol smiled. "Your face is dirty. Come wash up."

The children sat cross-legged on the floor, while Silas lounged in his chair before the fireplace, his sock feet propped on the stool in front of him.

"Jump, jump, jump. Now I get a crown?" Sara asked.

Josiah looked at the board in wonder. He exhaled, sputtering his lips in frustration, causing the hair on his brow to bounce.

"A quick learner she is, son?" Silas laughed. "Maybe tic-tac-toe would be more to your advantage," he teased.

Sara questioned, "Tic-tac-toe?"

Josiah rose from the floor to fetch a pad and pencil from the mantel. Sitting next to Sara, he drew a tic-tac-toe grid and placed an X in one corner. "Now you put an O anywhere," he instructed.

Sara placed her hands behind her back and shook her head.

"Come on," urged Josiah, "Just put an O in one of the squares. Then, I'll show you what comes next."

A frown creasing her forehead, Sara simply stared at him.

Silas placed his feet on the floor and leaned forward. "Do you know what an O is, Sara?"

Sara shook her head.

"Do you know how to read and write, child?"

Again, Sara shook her head.

"Well," Silas affirmed, "we have to fix that. Come here."

Sara stood and hesitated to approach him.

"Come, come, lass," he insisted.

Sara moved into his outstretched arms, and Silas set her on his knee.

"Sara, we are going to teach you to read and write. But, first, let's get this X and O business behind us, so you can best him at this, too." Silas tousled Josiah's hair and took the pad and pencil from him.

Josiah sat on his knees at his father's feet, while Sara had her first lesson.

* * * * * * * * *

The table was spread with fried fish, squirrel and dumplings, greens from the garden, and cornbread with fresh-churned butter. As if that were not fast enough, thought Nancy, there were fried apple pies for dessert. "Peggy," she concluded, "I have overfed myself! Thank you. The food couldn't have been better." Nancy squeezed Sara's knee under the table.

Sara's words were soft. "Thank you, Mrs. McKinnon. It was good."

Peggy smiled in response, as Carol added, "You have the skill of our mother, it seems, Peggy. I am reminded how much I enjoyed eating at her table."

"Well, I like to cook and feed appreciative eaters." Peggy stood as she gathered plates. "I'll clean up the dishes. You just rest and visit while I straighten up."

"Want to play tic-tac-toe?" Josiah whispered across the table.

Sara looked to Nancy for permission. She nodded, and the children hastened to their position in front of the opposing fireplace.

Silas's eyes followed Peggy as she bustled about the dining room, clearing the table, then settled herself in the kitchen. Silas took his pipe, tobacco pouch, and a tin from the mantle. He stuffed the bowl of the pipe, took a sliver of wood from the tin, scratched it on a stone of the fireplace, and flame burst from the end of it.

Silas noted Nancy raised her eyebrows in question and surprise. "A match," he said, holding the blazing splinter before him. "White phosphorous is coated on the end. Scratch it on just about anything, and it lights." Holding the flame above his pipe bowl, he inhaled the fire into the tobacco. When the aromatic smoke curled about his head to his satisfaction, he lowered his voice and asked, "Do you ladies mind telling me about your ordeal, or would it be too grievous?"

Carol deferred to Nancy for a reply.

Perhaps it was the evocative effect of the pipe smoke, perhaps the intensity and depth of concern in Silas's blue eyes— something assuaged the chilling pain in Nancy's chest and melted the icy lock upon her spirit and tongue. "My child was three months in the womb when the soldiers came. The crops were rising. I was sewing, and David had gone into the mountain to hunt."

With the unveiling of her memories before the ears of the gentle Scot came release. Peace pervaded her soul and brought light to the far, dark recesses of her mind, into which Nancy had pressed the anger and hatred that had been her real motivation since the removal. Doubtless, she was concerned for her child and for the birthright that had been ripped from him, but she realized she would not allow the soldiers victory—they would not have their way. Let them take the land; they could not take the fortitude and determination she would use to take some of it back with intelligent enterprise and diligent effort. Let them take her husband and half her heart; they could not take from her his memory, his legacy of courage and strength, his child.

Tears had dampened the bosom of her dress like raindrops, as she finished speaking. "I will build again—a home for me and my children—and for my friend for as long as she will stay." Nancy lowered her head, as Silas, with compassion, took her hand and pressed her fingers.

"Well, that was fast work now, wasn't it?" Peggy, drying her hands on her apron, stood at the entrance to the log cabin kitchen.

"Come, sit, Peg, and talk with us," he requested.

"No, Silas," she refused. "Seems you have enough talkers. I'll go up and see about fixing beds."

"If you don't mind, I'll go help Peggy," said Nancy. "I'm really very tired."

"Go right ahead," agreed Silas, then, teasing, "A thin reed like yourself has carried a fair size load quite a way."

Forcing a smile in return, Nancy patted her front and said, "Good night. Carol, will you see to Sara when you come to bed?"

"Surely."

Nancy turned at the hallway. "And you might speak to Silas about the plans we were discussing."

"I will," Carol assured her. "You two sleep well." she smiled.

"And sleep until you wake," added Silas.

"Thank you." She called to Sara, "Sara, come to bed when Carol says it's time."

"I will, Nancy," she responded without looking up from the tablet.

"It's your turn to make an X," Josiah instructed.

* * * * * * * * *

The shadows of evening were beginning to dim their sight. Silas made his nightly circuit of the house to light the oil lamps on the mantels, dining table and light stands, before resuming his seat and asking, "And what about you, Carol? How did you end up at the stockade? What was it like for you?"

She pondered, then spoke, "It was not such a surprising thing for me, I think. I stayed informed of the political situation and knew Jackson was a snake. They would take the land eventually, I believed. So, I prepared, worked each day as I had the day before, waited for them to come—which, they did."

Peggy entered the room, wiping the perspiration on her forehead with the sleeve of her dress, and said, "Well, Nancy is

61

settled on the cot that was up there, and I have made thick pallets for you and Sara. I think you will be comfortable."

Carol chuckled. "Our last night was spent on a limestone slab overlooking the valley. I think we will rest well."

Peggy sat at the table across from Carol. "And what have you been up to these many years, sister?"

"Little of consequence since I saw you last. Keeping the school open after Aunt Ethel died, keeping enough of the farm going to meet my needs and share a little."

"No man to share it with yet?" she probed.

"No." Carol's voice was calm as she reminded, "But now there is nothing left to share."

Peggy gave Carol's arm a light tap. "Oh, that's right. I'm sorry, I forgot. Well, Nancy says you are going to start over in Shake Rag."

Carol nodded and turned her attention to Silas. "Nancy has mentioned to you about finding a piece of land, Silas, and hiring your help with a cabin. What do you think about building a schoolhouse, too? Are their enough children in Shake Rag to make that worth considering?"

"I should say so! If there were none other than Sara and Josiah, that'd be plenty! And I tell you what—if Nancy likes the bit of land, I have in mind for her and the children, I'll give you a neighboring piece and build you a schoolhouse. And if you want a place of your own, I'll build you a house, too."

"Well, Silas, when are you going to find time to work and take care of your own family?" Peggy blurted.

Silas waved his pipe. "Look around you, Peg. Have I ever let you go hurting? There are plenty of hours in the day, and I can round up help if need be."

Carol protested, "Silas, Nancy has some money she had saved, but I just lived day to day. I can't afford to buy land, and I'll not sell my pride for it."

"Carol, your father let me buy all this for little more than the price of a good squirrel rifle. He was a good, generous man. He knew I didn't have much. I have taken what he gave me and made a fine living out of it. It's time for me to return the favor to you and Nancy."

Peggy looked grim and said nothing.

Carol fought back tears, then spoke with a choking voice, "You are a good and generous man, too, Silas. Thank you. Nancy will insist on paying you. She is a proud woman and wants to make her own way. I feel the same—but—perhaps, I can repay Nancy and you—and Peg—in care and schooling for the children."

Silas patted her hand. "If you can educate my boy and help him grow to be a man as fine as your father, I don't have enough land to repay you!"

The touch of his hand on hers wrenched her heart. The remembrance of Silas, his giant form draped across the body of her father, his friend, made her chest ache. Perhaps it was at that moment—when Silas's tears blessed the remains of the proud old chief, she had known she would love this man as long as she had breath and will.

Her eyes burning with restrained tears, Carol smiled her gratitude. "It has been a long, full day," she sighed. "I'd better get Sara to bed." She stood and extended her hand to Silas. "Thanks, again." Moving to the other side of the table, she placed her hands on her sister's shoulders. "Peggy, I will always be grateful for the way you have welcomed us into your home." She leaned down to place her cheek against her sister's. "I promise, we will be in our own place before we are dead fish!"

Silas added, "Carol, you and Nancy be ready after lunch tomorrow. I'll show you the property I have in mind. It's just back toward town a way. Sara and Josiah can ride with us in the back of the wagon."

"We'll be ready. Thanks." As Carol said, "Good night" from the hallway, Peggy's tense voice replied, "Sleep well."

* * * * * * * * *

Carol awoke to leaf shadows dancing in a shaft of sunlight on the wall before her. She had not moved since she lay on the pallet the previous night, and her mind groped toward the light her eyes perceived. Sitting up, cross-legged under the cover, elbows on her knees, she propped her head in her hands and cleaned the corners of her eyes with her little fingers.

Nancy was still asleep on the cot, and gentle snoring was coming from Sara on the floor at Nancy's foot. Carol dressed in her petticoat, skirt and bodice, picked up her boots, eased down the steps, and let herself out the back door to the outhouse and the spring.

Carol returned to find Peggy sitting at the table, as she had been when Carol had retired to bed. "Good morning," she greeted her sister. "Hope I'm not too late for a cup of coffee."

"No, there's a fresh pot on the stove. I figured you all would be getting up before long." Peggy did not move. "The cups are on the shelf."

Carol poured herself some coffee and sat across from Peggy. "I have not slept like that since leaving Stanley."

"Are the woman and the girl awake?" she asked.

Carol's eyebrow raised before answering, "No. They were sleeping like the dead when I slipped out. They each have been through a terrible time. I am glad they can rest."

"They'll have to be up and about soon, or they'll miss breakfast. I'll have to start lunch for Silas and Josiah."

"Peggy, besides expecting a child, Nancy has lost her husband, and Sara, her father. There have been many nights when their sleep was troubled or did not come at all. Thanks to you, they have a place where they can have some comfort. Don't worry about food."

"Did you know Nancy at Stanley?" Peggy asked.

"No. Didn't Silas tell you? We met at the stockade. She is our far cousin by marriage to David Hilderbrand. When he died, Sara looked through the stockade to see if anyone knew Nancy, if she had any family. I remembered our kinship, and we joined camps."

"Silas mentioned something about that." Peggy rose to get the pot to refresh her cup. "I've never kept up with the family ties the way you have. I likely wouldn't have recognized the name." Peggy took a cloth from the pan on the table. "Do you want a biscuit and bacon to go with that coffee?"

"That would be good. Thanks." She waited for Peggy to settle. "I see Silas has treated you well these last many years—this is a fine house."

"Yes, he is a good provider. The grist mill and saw mill are the only ones between the river and the Sequatchie. He has good business—he works long and hard."

"You have a fine son, too," added Carol.

"Yes, I do." Peggy smiled. "I am very proud of Josiah."

"I'm surprised you haven't filled this big house with more handsome sons and daughters in all these years," Carol probed.

"One pregnancy and birthing was all I could bear! You were the one made for childbirth—not me! I could not endure another ordeal like that—in labor a whole day—nearly split in half! Never again! I told Silas I would die if I had to go through that again."

"That's too bad." Carol thought of the father and son with so much love to give—for other children, for brothers and sisters.

66

"Silas would have had a half dozen by now, if he'd had his way—but not by me!" Peggy began clearing the table. She looked at Carol with a wry smile. "That's why I thought it curious he should bring home a child and a woman with another one on the way."

"Peggy! I hope you are not suggesting…"

"I'm just saying I thought it strange—your showing up here from Stanley, with those two, after all these years."

"Well, I hope you have a better understanding of things now," declared Nancy, just entering the doorway. Sara peeped from behind Nancy's skirt.

"Well, good morning, lazy heads!" Peggy's greeting was cheerful. "Just in time to have a bite of breakfast."

Nancy's look was withering, and Sara did not move.

Carol said, "Nancy, come have something to eat to hold you till lunch. Afterward, Silas is going to take us to look at the land he mentioned."

"Sara, sit down and eat," Nancy directed. "I'll join you in a few minutes." Nancy went toward the back door.

Carol rose to get another cup of coffee and refilled her own. She avoided her sister, as she ordered, "Peggy, see about some breakfast for the child."

Emotion tumbling and surging through her like the undercurrent flowing between the mountains, Nancy walked toward the river. Tears of anger and frustration stung her eyes. Without blinking, Peggy had opened her home with one hand and had slapped her guests with the other.

"Nancy!" Carol called.

Folding her arms around herself, Nancy stopped.

"Here, have a cup of coffee." Carol nudged Nancy's arm with the cup.

Nancy looked at the mug then took it, wrapping her hands around it.

"Welcome to the home of my sister. I warned you."

"We should leave," Nancy stated.

"And go where?" asked Carol.

Nancy had no answer.

"The only harm Peggy can do is the harm you allow her to do. You are strong, brave, smart, expecting a child—as pretty as Peggy—all the things she is not and the only thing she is. That is hard for her to take. Ignore her."

"But we are living under her roof! We are eating her food!" Nancy followed the beaten path closer to the water. "We should not have come."

"Yes, her care will fatten us, and her words will carve us up for stewing—but only if we let them. It is not that we are unwelcome—she just thrives on attention, and she gets little unless she causes conflict." Carol stood shoulder to shoulder with her friend. "Be polite but ignore. It is the only defense."

Nancy fixed her attention on Carol. "We will get out as soon as we can."

"All right but come back now and end Peg's gloating."

Nancy nodded and followed Carol back to the house.

Sara was eating a biscuit and having a cup of milk.

"You'll likely be needing some milk, too." Peggy directed her words toward Nancy and set another cup on the table."

"Thank you." Nancy words were soft, as she avoided Peggy's gaze. She directed her words to Carol, "So, you say we are going to look at some land after lunch?"

Carol nodded as she took another sip of coffee. "Silas said it's back toward town a bit."

Peggy interrupted, "The trail cuts through a good site about three-quarters of a mile back—has a stream running through it. Silas has already mostly cleared it. Bet that's what he's talking about."

Nancy glanced at Carol and commented, "I'm sure it will be just fine."

* * * * * * * * *

"The way I see it, we situate a cabin right about there, back in that grove of trees, as the trail crooks on that side." Silas closed his eyes and sighted the plot with his hands.

"Can we get out, Pa?" Josiah asked from the back of the wagon.

"Sure, go ahead. Show Sara the stream." Silas continued, "Then on over there," he gestured with his left hand to the other side of the trail, "as it turns back toward town, we could build the schoolhouse—within easy walking distance."

"It's a beautiful piece of land, Silas," Nancy observed, "but I'm not sure we can afford it."

"What are you looking to pay?" he asked.

"Fifty dollars is all I can afford, to have enough to buy supplies and fabric for sewing."

"Well, I'd be wanting a hundred." Silas's expression was serious.

Nancy's face was blank, but Carol knew her friend's insides were churning. Carol wondered where Silas was heading.

He was straightforward. "I'll take your fifty and, from Carol, I'll take fifty in barter for school-teaching the children. I'll throw in the building as my contribution to the community for having you all here." He grinned. "Deal?"

Nancy sighed and looked at Carol for agreement.

Carol laughed and said, "You've got my fifty!"

Nancy smiled and extended her hand to Silas. "Deal."

"Good. Now let's get out and walk you over your land." He circled the wagon to help them down, but Carol had alighted and was moving toward the location for the schoolhouse. "You can see what the schoolteacher's interested in!" He helped Nancy to the ground as he called after Carol, "You just best be getting some lessons ready for the children—I aim to have you open for business come fall!"

Silas was enthusiastic, as he explained his plan to Nancy. "I figure two good-size bedrooms upstairs. And you'll be needing a workroom for your sewing—a place where people can come and pick up their things without bothering you in the main part. We can put an ell with a door out this way off the downstairs."

Nancy was silent as she followed Silas and listened to his ideas, but her mind was racing in a confusion of sadness, relief, hope. She had lost so much, but so much was being returned to her— all except David. Part of her wanted to shout for joy, but, somehow, such happiness seemed to betray her husband.

"What do you think?" Silas asked.

It took a moment for his voice to reach Nancy's understanding. She looked at him, "I really don't know what to think." In response to his perplexed look, she explained, "So much has happened since the removal—losing David, losing our home, the misery of the stockade—then Sara, Carol, your family—now, all this. I can't seem to slow my mind down to take hold of it all."

Silas directed Nancy to a nearby stump. "Have a seat, lass, and rest yourself."

Nancy sat, pressed her hands on her knees, and arched her back to relieve the ache creeping up her spine.

Silas dropped on his haunches and removed a knife from his pocket. Picking up a twig, he began whittling. "The way I would see it, Nancy, you need to hold on to the memory of David and that happiness and let the rest go. Imagine him with you—looking over your shoulder, cheering you on."

71

Nancy smiled at the gentle bear crouching beside her. "How is it you seem to always to have the right words?"

"Talk's easy." He threw the twig and scoured the ground before finding another. "Unless you're trying to tell yourself something." He flashed a smile at her before saying, "I don't listen to myself too well."

Moving to less personal ground, Nancy said, "Silas, thank you for all your kindness. You have been so good and generous to me." She grinned. "My husband— who looks over my shoulder— and I can never express enough appreciation."

"I'm the one needs to be thanking you and Carol for coming here. I work from sunup to sundown to keep the mills going. I need a diversion, a project, something more to build." He swept the twig through the air. "This is it—a home, seamstress shop, and school for Shake Rag. We'll have the best dressed, most well-educated citizenry this side of Knoxville!"

Nancy laughed and declared, "Silas McKinnon, no one can accuse you of small-thinking!"

Silas blew a salute on the twig whistle he had made and extended his arm. "May I be escorting you now to the other side of the trail? I need to be giving Carol my grandiose ideas for her school building."

* * * * * * * * *

Sara and Josiah had doffed their shoes and stockings, and Carol watched as they waded and splashed in the spring that rolled down the mountain, across the trail, and through the property. Silas had put care and consideration into his offer and had presented it to them in such a way as to preserve their dignity. She was grateful for this. At times, she had felt like a parasite—first, on her aunt, then, on Nancy's back. Now, she would have a life and goals of her own—true, through the benevolence of Silas, but still, a life in which she could make her own way through diligence and devotion to teaching.

And she would have to be dedicated to her work, if she was to be content in this place. Silas and Josiah belonged to Peggy, who could never appreciate how richly she had been blessed. That thought she must put far from her mind—that ground contained traps and pitfalls she must avoid.

Carol jumped at the sound of Silas's voice behind her.

"Sorry to have startled you," he apologized. "We laid out our plans for the house and thought we'd size up the school building next."

"You're moving right along!" she laughed.

Silas shouted above the gurgling tumble of water to the sounds of happy children, "You're making that look pleasant enough; I just might join you!"

"Come in!" cried Sara, giggling.

"Come in, Pa! We've got a crawdad!" chimed Josiah.

"I'll leave him to you, son!" Silas said, "Come, Carol, if you're not inclined to go wading, let me tell you what I have in mind for the school building."

As Silas spoke about his proposed Shake Rag Community School, Carol envisioned the structure with a throng of students, eager to learn and to be together in their own special place—she would make it so. "…only a couple or three months to get it finished," she heard Silas say.

"For the schoolhouse?" she asked.

"For everything!" he responded. "We'll get the house up first, then still have plenty of time before the crops are in to get the school building finished. I've got some workers I can spare who'll help. We'll have you settled before you know it."

"That would be very good," said Nancy. "I'm afraid we are going to be a burden to Peggy. I'd like to get in our own place soon."

"Now, Nancy, don't you go worrying about Peg." He jested, "All she has to do is fix a bit extra for two skinny women and a child." He looked at Nancy's abdomen, raised his eyebrows, and added, "Make that a child and a half—who don't eat much and take up leftover floor space."

"Well, Silas, I must say, I never felt less like a burden—and more like a rug!" Carol teased.

Silas laughed and clapped his hands. "Good. Now, let me drop you all at the store for a bit, while I see to some business. Then, we'll head back to the house." Silas called the children, "Josiah, you and Sara get your boots on and load up. We're going into town."

* * * * * * * * * *

Silas had explained that the landing store, originally just a shack on the riverbank to service the keelboats making their way to Muscle Shoals, had grown with the community and had moved across the river trail to service a larger clientele. The nearest competitor being over the mountain at Stanley, the store had become a focal point of social life, the primary disseminator for news and gossip, and the assembly place when the occasional circuit rider came their way.

Mounting the entrance steps, Nancy told Sara, "You and Josiah may each pick out some candy, as long as you save it till after supper." The children scurried to examine the supply of sweets in front of the counter, behind which a lady was arranging canned goods on a shelf.

"Good afternoon, ladies. How are you all today?" The woman turned from her work to greet them. She reminded Nancy of a plump hen, as her shirtwaist covered a generous bosom and thick waist and drooped in folds over narrow hips. Her nose hooked a bit at the tip, and coarse red hair sprouted from the part leading to the loose bun at the nape of her neck. "I'm Elizabeth Wilmouth," she introduced herself. "My husband and I own the store."

Nancy moved to extend her hand to Mrs. Wilmouth. "I am Nancy Hilderbrand. My daughter and I are staying with Silas and Peggy McKinnon. This is Peggy's sister, Carol Hicks." Nancy noticed Elizabeth Wilmouth's tanned hand and cheeks, and the depth of her dark chocolate eyes.

"Good to have you in Shake Rag. Planning on staying with us?" she inquired.

Recognizing a potential source of advertisement, Nancy replied, "Yes, we have just agreed to buy a piece of land from Mr. McKinnon. I am a widow. I plan to build on the land. I am a seamstress by trade. If you have any need for sewing work, please keep me in mind. Or, if you know anyone who does, I would appreciate your passing along my name.

"Why, sure, Mrs. Hilderbrand."

"Nancy," she interjected.

"Sure, Nancy, I'll keep that in mind. And we can order whatever fabric or notions you need—right down from Ross's Landing, Knoxville—even Cincinnati, if we need to. We keep a few things in stock—some basics, local homespun—back there against the far wall."

"Thank you. I'll be giving you plenty of business, I hope." Nancy turned Elizabeth's attention to the children. "Mind giving each of them a penny's worth when they make up their minds?" Nancy laid the coins on the counter and moved to scout out the notions.

Carol found only a meager stock of writing materials and glanced through a few newspapers and a handful of outdated periodicals. "Mrs. Wilmouth, we are going to try to get a school set up for the community by fall. Would you be able to order books and supplies for us?"

"A school—here in Shake Rag? You don't mean it!"

"Yes, ma'am, we've located property, and my brother-in-law has offered to build the school house."

"Well, if that ain't the answer to prayer! I was just telling my husband the other day how we need a school in these parts—nearest one's over at Stanley."

"I'm afraid the one at Stanley's no longer open," Carol countered.

"You don't say?"

"No, ma'am, I was the teacher there—followed my aunt. The school building was on her property, and the soldiers confiscated the land, the school—just about everything, when they removed the Cherokee from their homes at Stanley."

"Well, I can't tell you how sorry I am." Carol could see the sincerity in Elizabeth's dark eyes turn to remorse as she added, "I have family I haven't seen since I married Mr. Wilmouth, going on twenty years ago now. If they're still alive, they're likely in the West by now—or worse, penned up in some stockade like animals awaiting slaughter."

"This is a sad and terrible time for our people," Carol responded.

Elizabeth questioned, "How did you come to be here, if the soldiers moved you out?"

There was a slight tilt to the corners of her mouth, as Carol responded, nodding toward Nancy. "With the help of my brave friend and the carelessness of some drunken guards, we managed to get out of the stockade at Ross's Landing. Nancy and I are greatly blessed to have made our way here, to the home of my sister."

Elizabeth said, "Well, I should say—" Glancing over Carol's shoulder, she exclaimed, "Peggy, we've just been speaking of you!"

Peggy entered the doorway with basket in hand. "Thought I felt my ears tingling a bit, Elizabeth. And what have my houseguests been telling you about me?"

"Just about how they come all the way from Ross's Landing to be with you —and about our new school that's intended." Turning back to Carol, Elizabeth added, "I can hardly wait to tell Mr. Wilmouth and some of my friends with children. We'll have you a passel of young'uns come fall, Miss Carol! I can guarantee you that!"

"That husband of mine sure gets all kinds of grand ideas now, doesn't he?" Peggy shook her head with a grimacing smile. "We'll just have to wait and see what comes of it, Elizabeth, before you go and get everyone all excited." Peggy scooped a bag of coffee beans, tied it, and placed it on the counter.

"Peg, you should have come in the wagon—no need to walk," observed Carol.

"The wagon looked pretty full to me!" she retorted. "Besides, you all were going to be tied up looking at land, and I needed to get back in time to fix your supper." Peggy observed the children at the candy bins and spoke to her son, "Josiah, you need to come on home with me now."

"But, Pa's going to come back for us in the wagon," he protested.

"Don't argue, Josiah. We'll be home long before they get back, and I need your help."

Josiah's frowning face turned toward Sara, and he rolled his eyes. "Yes, ma'am."

Peggy breathed a deep sigh, covered her brow with her hand, and said to the storekeeper, "My, this heat just saps a person! I just seem to be worn out all the time lately." She laughed. "Better let me have another bottle of that tonic you been pushing, Elizabeth."

"Oh, it'll do you wonders, Peggy! Just give it time."

"Well, put one in." Peggy turned again toward Josiah. "Leave that sack of candy with Carol," she ordered.

Josiah handed the sack to his aunt and followed his mother to the exit.

Peggy called over her shoulder, "I'll get your supper ready. You girls try to have Silas home before dark."

August 1838

By Silas's order, Carol, Nancy, and Sara had awakened with the chickens. Today, he had said, would be the unveiling of a great surprise at the new house, and he wanted them all there early.

Carol set her boots by the table and proceeded into the kitchen, where Peggy stood at the wash basin. "Good morning, Peg, are Silas and Josiah already gone?"

Peggy jumped. "You startled me!" She turned and chirped, "Why, my, yes! Aren't they always up and about with the sun these days?"

Nancy and Sara were close on Carol's heels. "Peg don't bother about breakfast for us," Nancy said. "We'll just have some coffee, and Sara may want some milk. We'll carry some biscuits with us."

"Silas sure has you all on the move today," she observed, as she poured coffee into the cups on the table. "What's going on over there?"

Carol asked in reply, "Hasn't he told you?"

Peggy chuckled, "Silas doesn't tell me his plans—I hardly see him these days!" Peggy set the milk pitcher on the table and reached for a cup from the shelf. She poured it full, but before she could hand it to Sara, it slipped from her fingers and shattered on the plank flooring. "Land sakes! Now look at that mess I've made for myself!"

Sara scurried to pick up the shards.

"Get out of the way, child! I'll do it myself!" Peggy waved Sara away.

Sara jumped back against Nancy's skirt.

"Peg, she was just going to help," chided Carol.

"You all can just go along and get out of my way—that'll help!" Her apron skirt swinging like a pendulum from her waist, Peggy ignored them as she crawled around the broken pieces and sopped up milk with her dishtowel.

The morning was clean and fresh, the trail beneath the trees shaded and free of the oppressive heat that would stifle the valley later in the day. The women walked in silence, until Sara spoke, "Wonder what kind of surprise Uncle Silas has for us?"

"'Uncle Silas?'" Nancy questioned.

Carol explained, "Silas told Sara the next best thing to a father is an uncle and for her to call him 'Uncle.'"

Sara's smile was wide with pleasure.

Nancy admitted, "Well, that has a nice sound— 'Uncle Silas.'" She continued, "Whatever it is, I'm sure it will be a nice surprise—Uncle Silas has been full of nice surprises!"

Sara skipped ahead, stopping at times to investigate wildflowers, stones, or other potential treasures along the way.

Nancy asked, in a subdued voice, "Peggy is not well, is she?"

Sarcasm dripped from Carol's whispered response. "She should be healthy as a horse with all the tonic she's been taking!"

Nancy was surprised, and Carol scolded, "You're the one with all the knowledge of natural healing—haven't you noticed the signs? Peg even smells of it at times."

"I guess I've been preoccupied with the house. I just thought she might be ill."

Carol shook her head. "Call it 'homebrew' and people say 'Shame, shame'; call it 'tonic' and they say, 'Drink up, it'll cure your ailments.'"

"I wonder if Silas knows," Nancy mused.

"I would say so. Might explain why we he's working the way he does. I'll never understand why Peg must make the worst of things." Carol said no more, and they continued their trek in silence.

The bustling activity of building at the house seemed to have diminished, and no one was in sight as the women approached. Sara had run ahead and was already inside, as Carol and Nancy mounted the steps to the porch. Just as they reached the portal, the door swung back and Sara, beaming, announced, "It is a surprise!"

Drying his hands on a filthy rag, Silas appeared, towering over Sara from behind. A streak of black grease slashing his brow, nose and right cheek, he apologized, "I'd take your hands and escort you in, but, as you can see, I'm a might dirty."

"Come see!" Sara raced to the kitchen off the main room.

Carol and Nancy caught up to the child to find her on a crate she had pulled in front of the sink. Turning a handle on a pipe entering the outside wall above the basin, she then clasped her hands, hugged them to herself with joy, and watched for their reaction as a fall of water tumbled from the conduit.

"No more carrying those heavy buckets from the spring!" Silas announced. "I ran pipe right from it into the house. Pull the plug and another pipe carries the wash water back out into the yard."

"Oh, Silas! Thank you!" exclaimed Carol.

Nancy observed the cascade of water, then moved to extend her arms to the fall. She filled her cupped hands and drank. "As cold and sweet as if it were flowing right through the kitchen."

"Well, it is, lass—straight from the spring and into your sink!"

Nancy's voice was soft. "Silas, it is such a good thing— thank you."

Peggy's rancorous voice sounded behind them, "Yes, Silas, such a good thing—thank you! Shame you couldn't have thought of your own family first." Her eyes were red, and Nancy thought she must have been crying.

Silas went to his wife. "Now, Peg, don't feel bad. I'm going to run a pipe from our spring to your kitchen, too."

"Now you are!"

"No, I have had all the materials. I've had this planned for us. I just needed to make sure I got all the fittings right. Carol and Nancy weren't going to be needing their kitchen yet—I figured I try it out here first, then do ours when I knew I had it working properly."

Peggy just glared at Silas in disbelief.

"Come on, Peg, let's take you home. I've got to get cleaned up and take care of some business." He turned back to the women at the sink. "You ladies look around. I think you're about ready to move in. If there's anything you see needs doing, let me know." Silas took Peggy's arm and led her to the wagon waiting outside. "Oh, Sara!" he called, "Josiah went walking up the stream a way. Why don't you go look him up and make sure he comes back when you all do."

Nancy hastened to the porch and said, "Silas, Peggy's not feeling well. Let her rest. We'll fix us all a nice supper—our last one together for a while. We'll be moving tomorrow, since it looks like you have everything ready."

Silas assisted Peggy into the wagon as Nancy spoke.

Carol stood behind Nancy. She watched Silas as he heard Nancy's words. She saw the grim line of his mouth and the twitch of his eyes at the corners where they had been crinkled by lines of laughter. She knew he was embarrassed and stinging with anger at her sister's behavior.

Silas seated himself on the buckboard, picked up the reins, and caught her eyes, peering over Nancy's shoulder. In the flash of the silent, yet eloquent moment, Carol understood his misery, his loneliness—his penitence. She knew words would never be spoken, but the communication between them would be sufficient to sustain her and to assuage the desire for justice she had denied yet harbored. All those years ago, his choice of Peggy had been a knife thrust into her heart, then twisted again and again with every thought of it. But

Silas was paying for his choice each day of his life—and while she loved him and grieved for him, a part of her pain was eased with the awareness that he suffered and sorrowed.

September 1838

A wide shaft of hazy sunlight penetrated the stillness of the early morning and urged Nancy to open her eyes to the mid-September morning. The baby, finally quiet after tumbling and bouncing off the inside of her taut abdomen for many hours of the night, was asleep, and she had sunk into clouds of soft slumber and dreams of David. Nancy blinked as she struggled to recognize and cross the boundary between the reality of sleep and the tangible cubicle of space in which she lay.

The loft room was like that of the cabin she had shared with David, but Silas had made it twice the size to allow room for the cradle and another bed as the child grew. A similar room on the other side of the stairwell to the first floor was shared by Carol and Sara and already contained two beds. At some time, the children would share the room, and Carol would move to her own compact, but sufficient quarters off the school building.

Nancy shifted her massive middle to the bedside, placed her feet on the floor, and sat, contemplating the room, the cabin, the land, and the day to come, while she willed herself to stand. David, always in her heart and mind, and now in her dreams—it seemed, nightly—urged her to move forward, to work, to make a good life for herself and the child. *Ah, the child*, she thought. *Nearly two moons, at least!* Surely there was a limit to the expanse of her body!

Nancy looked out the window of the room and saw workers already at the schoolhouse, in the clearing where the trail curved westward. They were unloading more furnishings and supplies, she reckoned. If the children of Shake Rag remained untaught, it would not be due to lack of materials—Silas McKinnon was seeing to that!

Nancy knew the money she had paid Silas for the land and for his help could not approach the investment he had made in their settlement. The tracts he had offered were about halfway between the McKinnon home place and town. Nancy had bought the piece farther to the east, set back in a grove of hardwoods, with a level garden spot and room for a cow and a few chickens. The school building was on the opposite side of the trail and closer to town by three hundred yards. Silas had worked from the early mists of dawn to the chirping sounds of night to attend to his own chores and to the work of the mills, while overseeing every joint in every structure on the women's properties. From the spring running between the tracts, he had even piped water to the schoolhouse as he had to Nancy's cabin.

As Nancy started to lift her dress from the hook by the window, she saw Peggy entering the schoolyard. She saw her speak to one of the workers as he was sliding what looked like a chalkboard toward the rear of the wagon. The man motioned to the side of the building, and Peggy followed his direction but stopped as she met Silas coming around the schoolhouse. Nancy noticed their conversation was animated—Peggy was weaving, and her arms flailed before coming to rest on her hips. She could not see

Silas's face, but he seemed to respond with anger, just before Peggy whirled, staggered, bumped into a sawhorse, then stomped away, retreating in her tracks.

Nancy had not seen Peggy much since their move to the new house, but Josiah had come almost every day to help Silas as he could or just to play with Sara. Nancy was pleased Sara had a friend her own age—she seemed to have regained some of the innocence and joy of childhood since they had been at Shake Rag. Nancy hoped whatever problem Peggy might be having would not disrupt the harmony and peace Nancy desired for her family. *Perhaps*, she thought, *the less contact with Peggy, the better.*

A rumble of activity and voices downstairs encouraged Nancy to move along with her dressing. Nancy tucked one of David's handkerchiefs under her sleeve at the wrist and waddled her way to the bottom of the stairs. Smelling the welcoming aromas of breakfast, she realized she was famished.

"Good morning!" Carol greeted her. "Are you hungry? Sara and I have made a feast fit for a day of celebration!" Sara's smile was wide in agreement.

"And what are we celebrating today? We have had many days of celebration, it seems, in the last several weeks." Nancy pulled a ladder-back chair from the table and lowered herself to the rush seat.

"Silas said the schoolhouse will be completed today, and everything will be ready for students to come—after the baby and the crops are in, of course." Carol placed a pan of biscuits on the table in front of Sara.

"You make it sound as if the baby's growing in a field," Nancy teased, causing them to laugh. "And, lately, at times, I wish he were!"

"You've not told us if you have decided on a name for the baby," reminded Carol, nudging Sara with her elbow to get her attention, "but I'm sure it's not going to be Cornflower or Squash Blossom."

Sara giggled, "Or Bean Pod, if it's a boy."

Nancy looked at them with a wry smile. "No, I think it might be Weed or Clover!"

Carol laughed into her apron, and Sara repeated with delight, "Weed or Clover!"

When they were seated before their breakfast of eggs, fried fat back and biscuits, they held hands and bowed their heads in silent thanks, as had been David and Nancy's custom. Nancy wanted her children to recognize and honor the One who had sustained them—the Giver—Jehovah, as David had called Him. She believed He held her husband to His bosom, while bringing them to this place of safety and friendship.

Nancy downed several bites to ease her hunger, then said, "I think the child will be called David Ross, if it is a boy—after his father, of course." She now was able to speak of David without the pain in her chest that left her breathless. "But then after John Ross, who fought for us to the very end."

"A fine name!" Carol remarked. "It sounds so strong and wise."

Sara broke the silence, "And what if it's a girl baby? I would like it to be a girl baby."

"A baby doll for you?" Nancy teased. "Well, if it is a girl, I think she will be named Margaret—Margaret Kaquoli, because I like the name Margaret and after the old friend I met in the stockade." Nancy placed her hand over Carol's. "The nearest to a sister I ever had."

Sara made them laugh again when she said, "I think I like 'Clover' better."

As Carol poured a second cup of coffee for Nancy and one for herself, Sara asked, "May I go see the schoolhouse? I finished my breakfast, and the bedroom is already straightened."

Nancy asked, "Do you have any chores that need doing?"

Sara looked at Carol for an answer.

Carol replied, "I think I can do without her this morning, if she'll get back in time to do a few things for me before lunch."

Nancy said, "Go ahead but don't get in the way—and don't wander off."

"Yes ma'am," Sara agreed, before unlatching the door, exiting, and easing it shut behind her. Her footsteps then pounded in a gallop across the porch and down the steps.

Carol laughed and sat again at her place. "It's good to see the child as she is now. I know there are times at night when she cries for her father, but most of the time she is happy."

"I'm afraid your sister is not happy. I saw, from the window this morning, what looked like a disagreement between her and Silas."

Carol shook her head, her lower lip curled under in frustration. "Silas is not spending enough time with her, she thinks. She said as much to me when I took her the clothes you repaired. Of course, as usual, she was laid up in the bed, suffering from her incurable ailment."

"Silas does spend long days at work—hard work," Nancy observed. "He seems driven to do or to oversee everything himself." She was quick to add, "Not that I don't appreciate his fine work and attention to detail—but, regardless of her odd way, I do see where she might feel neglected."

Carol studied the coffee in the cup before her, then spoke. "Silas is always looking to help others. He is a giver with a large heart, especially," she smiled, "for children and expectant mothers." Then, Carol's eyes were hard. "Peggy is a taker—like the eddy in the river, she will suck up and hold whatever comes near." Carol sighed. "Yes, Silas is a hard worker, a busy man—perhaps, driven by the fear of being caught in the undertow."

Nancy was disturbed. "I just don't understand Peggy, I guess."

Carol collected their cups, as she responded, "You don't know Peggy well yet. Peggy is competing with every other woman to be the center of attention—to be the prettiest, the wealthiest— even, the sickest, if need be." As she moved toward the sink, Carol added, "Just remember, Peggy will say or do anything, so keep your guard up."

"Why have Silas and Peggy had no more children?" Nancy asked above the sound of the water flowing from the new faucet.

"Josiah was a large baby. The birthing was painful but without complications. She just didn't want to go through it again." Carol dried the dishes and placed them on the shelf above the sink. "I feel sure Silas could not have too many children. Would give him a few more helping hands, now, wouldn't it?"

Nancy grimaced and stretched. "If you're finished, why don't we take a walk up to the schoolhouse ourselves?" she suggested, rubbing the small of her back. "Now that this child has stopped threatening me with his kicking, I need to work out some soreness. I was fearful he would break a rib, but finally he's settled down."

Carol hung the dishtowel on the peg under the shelf, threw her apron over the nearest chair, and retrieved a basket from the mantle. She teased, "Are you still enough Cherokee woman to walk to the landing store, or do you need to take to your bed?"

Nancy rose to her feet with the challenge. "Let's see if you can stay abreast of me!"

The women ascended the two steps to enter the schoolhouse, a one-room structure, about sixteen feet square, with a six by eight shed at the back. Silas—perspiration soaking his white shirt, sleeves rolled up to his elbows, and dripping from the thin ringlets encircling his fleshly nob like a crown, was in the process of setting a wood burning stove in the corner near the opening to the storage room, while his helpers—two of the free blacks, whom he had hired to help at the mills, attached the chalk board to a side wall. An alternating succession of tables and benches, two columns of four each, marched from front to back in the room.

"Good morning!" Carol called out to the workers.

"Morning, ma'am," one of the hired men responded. The other tipped his hat and nodded to each of them.

"Nancy! Carol! I'm glad you came!" Silas stood, his weight supported by a shiny black stove. "What do you think of this?" He gestured with his wrench. "All the way from Cincinnati? I thought if I put it in this corner, it would warm the storage room—if you ever used it as sleeping quarters." With a flourish of his arms, he directed their view to the left, then moved to follow their gaze. "And take a look at the chalkboard—low enough for the smallest," he stooped low, "and high enough for the tallest." He stood tall and measured his eye level with the board.

The women began to laugh at his enthusiastic presentation.

"Ah, ladies, but that's not all! Please notice our fine, smooth oak tables and benches, of graduated heights, front to back—ink wells set in place. "He pointed to the wall behind them. "On each side of the door, we have pegs and shelves for coats, lunch baskets, so forth." In a lowered, almost reverent voice, Silas said, "And, now, if you ladies will come right over here to this wall." He gestured to the fourth wall to their right. What appeared to be rolled canvas, strapped like a fabric log and hung by iron hooks, stretched across the upper middle third of the width. Silas held the roll in the center and released the straps at each end, then the middle strap, and allowed the canvas to unroll.

"Silas, maps!" Carol exclaimed, as Nancy's eyes opened wide.

"Yes, Carol, maps! Why, the la-di-da Commonwealthers don't have maps any finer than these!"

Nancy moved closer to examine the drawings, as Carol continued, "Silas, you have outdone yourself! You may have to find a teacher to measure up to all this!"

"No, no, lass, all this had to be worthy of the teacher who's come our way," he insisted. Silas noticed his helpers, having completed their securing of the chalkboard, were looking at the display opposite them. Silas motioned to them. "Tobias, Benjamin, come on over here and see these."

"What is this?" asked Nancy, as her fingers skimmed the veins and arteries of rivers and boundaries of territories.

"Well, this map is one of all the continents—the whole world. See, here's the United States—New York, Virginia. Here we are—Tennessee. There's Europe over there—and Scotland, where I was born. Benjamin, Tobias, there's Africa, land of your people. Now, pull up the leather loops on the corners down here and hook them up, and again the loops here on the back. Now, we see a map of just the United States and the western territories. Then, we can hitch this map up like the first, and we have the State of Tennessee. There's the river curving down and back up. Here's Ross's Landing, the Narrows—we'd be about right here." Silas jabbed the spot, as Nancy traced the course of the river.

"Silas, I hope the children are as excited about these, as I am," Carol enthused. "Do you have any idea how many children we'll have?"

"Well, Sara and Josiah, of course. I figure about eight, maybe ten more with Benjamin's two—you figure on letting your kids come, don't you, Ben?"

"Sir?"

"To school, man—you're going to send your kids to school, aren't you?"

"Well, sir, I don't rightly know," he stammered. "I didn't figure on it."

"Benjamin, your children need an education, just like all the rest. You have them here when the door opens," Silas ordered.

Benjamin studied Silas, then a smile spread across the dark face, and he responded, "Yes, sir. I reckon that'll be just fine. I'll see they're here."

Nancy's soft voice brushed their ears in the stillness that followed. "This was our land—the land my father gave us." Her hand seemed to be laying a gentle blessing on the map, where it depicted a boot-shaped thrust of earth, around which the river folded back on itself as it circuited the mountains.

Silas alone was able to find words to respond. "You know, Nancy, we're made of dust, and to dust we return. Maybe that's why our hearts get all tangled up in the soil, especially when we've known love and happiness on it."

Nancy could not look at Silas, but she smiled through misty eyes and nodded in agreement.

"Well, Silas, we're on our way to the landing store," stated Carol, tugging at Nancy's elbow. "We best be going. Silas, thank you, again, for everything. Tobias, Benjamin, thank you."

Benjamin said, "Our pleasure, ma'am," as Tobias smiled and tipped his hat again.

"No need for further thanks," claimed Silas. "We'll be taking our payment in teacher toil!" He saluted with his wrench and laughed at his own joke.

At the door, Nancy asked, "By the way, have you seen Sara?"

"I think you'll find her out back with Josiah." He added with a wink, "Quite a pair, those two!"

* * * * * * * * *

Carol had felt displaced, with a lack of purpose, since the Removal. Perhaps, she thought that was why Shake Rag had drawn her, despite its potential for sorrow. Carol knew she could be a solid, dependable rock, but she needed a place to settle—perhaps to grow old, scarred and covered with moss, but to be a stable and sure support for those she loved. Helping Nancy and caring for Sara had eased the sense of aimlessness, but the feeling of dependency on her friend, on Silas and, especially, on Peggy had wearied her soul.

She looked up at the azure sky and breathed in the freshness of the breeze off the mountainside. The school was changing everything. Carol felt renewed, vibrant, and eager to begin her own life. The children would be her purpose. She would teach them to read, to write, to use mathematical processes; but, more importantly, she would take the wisdom of the Ancient Ones and the best of the ways of the whites and forge a new path of learning. She would teach the children to hold to the ageless path of truth, justice, and reverence for the gifts of the Giver, while striving for a knowledge and understanding of the ever-changing world. She would instill in them, not the vision of manifest destiny which propelled the whites to plunder and seize what was not rightfully theirs, but a vision which would propel them to seize opportunities and to reach for heights limited only by their own desires and imaginations.

Carol recognized she would need to grow with the children. Resisting the uncertainties of the future, she had clung to the old ways. But the Removal had changed that—stripping away the veneer of favor with the Giver and oneness with his creation, leaving hearts naked to perish with the elements, to decay with the rottenness of hatred, or to harden in the fires of anger. She would choose to live without bitterness. She would teach the children not to cling to what was lost, but to what might be gained by education, industry, looking to the future, and overcoming the only real barriers—doubt and fear.

And Carol was happy that she shared this project with the only man she might ever love. Gone were the romantic notions of the young Kaquoli and the dreams of children of her own; any sadness or regret had been overshadowed by their eagerness and enthusiasm for the school. The union of their skills would bring into existence a place of learning and preparation for many children. Each year there would be a rebirth of students ready to accomplish new goals, new levels of mastery, or to dip their toes for the first time in the spring of learning Carol and Silas had tapped—a spring that might flow into a wide river and, thence, into an endless sea.

"Carol! Nancy! Look!" Sara's voice called to them as they rounded the corner of the schoolhouse.

In the shade of the towering hardwoods hedging the clearing behind the building, Silas had made a play area for the children—a couple of teeter-totters, a collection of wooden crates, and three rope swings, two of which were occupied by Josiah and Sara. Josiah was testing his strength by pulling himself up on a rope, while Sara, fearless, was pumping her legs and sailing through the air, as she tried to touch the branches.

"I feel like a bird!" she cried.

"You are going so high. Please, be careful," admonished Carol.

"Do you remember being so young?" asked Nancy.

"Perhaps," she replied. They watched the children for a few moments, and then Carol added, "I think I will come up here sometime and try that for myself."

Nancy chuckled and suggested, "We'd better go on to the store so we can get back to prepare lunch."

* * * * * * * * * *

Nancy enjoyed their excursions to the store. Mr. Wilmouth's stock was minimal, but Nancy was able to order a sufficient variety of fabrics from the dry goods store in, what the *Gazette* now called, "Chattanooga." Nancy wanted to be a regular face around Wilmouth's to publicize her presence in the community as a seamstress. Already, she had acquired some repair work and had made a welcoming dress for the Wilmouths' new granddaughter.

"Ah, Miss Nancy, how you be today?"

Nancy smiled and nodded.

"And Miss Carol, how's the schoolhouse coming along?" Mr. Wilmouth was a wiry, stooped fellow not much taller than Nancy herself. Icy blue eyes danced beneath his heavy gray brows as he darted from shelf to shelf—always crouched and ready to spring, like a gray squirrel, it seemed to Nancy.

Carol responded, "We'll be ready to call for our students as soon as the crops are in."

"Good, good." Wilmouth now seemed preoccupied, as he perched on his stool and searched in a barrel overflowing with a precarious pile of baskets, meal sacks, baling cord, and newsprint. "Here it is! Miss Nancy, I have something for you. I see you coming, and Elizabeth's been wanting me to give this to you."

She took the magazine from his hand.

"It's that lady's quarterly she told you about—from her sister in Cincinnati. Shows all the latest women's clothes they're wearing back East. She thought you might get some ideas from it, you bein' such a seamstress and all."

"Thank you, Mr. Wilmouth, and thank Elizabeth for me, too." Nancy's reservation disguised her excitement over seeing the elegant fashion plates. "May I sit back here and look at it?" She motioned behind the counter to the chair adjacent to his stool.

"Sure, have a seat."

Carol tapped her on the shoulder. "Nancy, I'm going to gather up a few supplies. You rest a bit."

Wilmouth slapped the dust off the chair with his hand. "How much longer you going to be carrying that load? My daughter was about your size the day Sally was born."

Carol, restraining her laughter, looked back at Nancy, who was embarrassed by his directness but amused by his honest expression of concern. "I think it will be several weeks yet," she answered.

The storekeeper shook his head and whistled, before scurrying away to help Carol.

Nancy turned the pages of the periodical until she came to the illustrations. The colors, the sweep of the gowns from the lithe figures set her imagination awhirl. She remembered the feel of the blue silk in her fingers, the weight of the folds in her lap, the rustling of the material as her knees moved against it. She knew she had the ability to give life to these pictures—not here, where there were few who had resources or concern for such things, but, perhaps, at Ross's Landing— "Chattanooga," she reminded herself. With its port and stagecoach route—and, now, talk of the railroad's extending into the town, the place was a prime location for the emergence of a social circle of wealthy ladies who would require such finery. Some already knew her there—among them, the lady who, perhaps, was still mourning over the Removal because it resulted in the loss of her blue silk.

"She said Silas comes home some nights smelling of whiskey. She doesn't know where he's been." The hushed voices speaking Silas's name broke Nancy's reverie. The women had mounted the porch steps and stood with their heads together outside the doorway. A bonnet turned as if one glanced inside, but she could not see Nancy seated behind the counter.

"John says Silas has been keeping long hours up there at his sister-in-law's, working on the schoolhouse," said another voice.

"Peggy says the schoolhouse is finished. Silas comes home to eat supper with Josiah, does his chores, and takes off again."

"You don't reckon he's stealing chickens from someone else's coop?"

The bonnet turned from side to side, "Who's to know? But it seems kind of peculiar about that Hilderbrand woman showing up—pregnant out to here, the way she did. Peggy said Silas practically gave her that ground."

Nancy's chest was heavy with the weight of their words; she struggled to draw breath into her lungs to clear her mind.

Carol approached the counter as Nancy rose to her feet and proceeded toward the door.

"Nancy?"

Nancy ignored her and followed the sound of the voices. With the bearing and backbone of one hardened by injustice and emboldened by opportunity, Nancy drew the attention of the startled women. With anger roiling beneath her placid countenance, like turbulence under the river sleeks, Nancy declared, "I am Nancy Hilderbrand, wife of David Hilderbrand, who was killed during the Removal from our land. My child—David's child, will be born in a place of peace and safety, thanks to the kindness and generosity of Silas McKinnon. He accepted what I had to pay, because it was all that I had. I will support myself and my child by my work as a seamstress—and I am a skillful seamstress." Gathering her skirts around her to move past the gossips, she descended the steps, then turned to add, "Come see me when you are in need of expert needlework." She called behind her, "Carol, you'll catch up to me on the trail."

The overbalancing of extra weight did not impede Nancy's charge toward home, and Carol, goods rattling in her basket, ran into puffs of dust stirred up in front of her.

"Nancy, wait up!" Her cry did not deter Nancy's eastward march.

As they came shoulder to shoulder, Carol panted, "Nancy, what happened back there? Are you all right?"

"I am beginning to understand about your sister." Nancy's voice was a husky tremor.

"What do you mean? What happened? Tell me!" she pled.

"Later."

They marched in silence along the river trail.

Passing the schoolhouse, Carol broke rank to tell Sara to come home when Silas and the workers left for lunch.

She anticipated following Nancy into the confines of their cabin, where she could settle Nancy with a cup of cold water, and the quiet routine of meal preparation would ease Nancy's tension and her tongue to tell her the troublesome matter. But Nancy kept on walking past the cabin. Carol sensed her friend was on a mission. The part of her that was seized by the impulse to restrain Nancy was overcome by the remembrance of Nancy's indomitable fortitude and will—and Carol smiled. She would wait at home, eager to hear the battlefield report.

* * * * * * * * *

Nancy sorted her thoughts as she trudged toward the McKinnons'. The fire in her soul and the child in her womb kept her weary body moving. She would not be threatened or intimidated by the insinuations of a sick, idle, self-consumed mind. She would teach her child, even now, not to cower, not to run, not to feel shame unless worthy of it, and not to bend against the wind, but to lean headlong into it.

Nancy rounded the fence-corner at the McKinnons' and strode up the porch to pound on the door.

Several seconds elapsed before Nancy heard footsteps approaching and Peggy opened the door.

"Well, Nancy, didn't expect a visit from you this morning." Peg's hair was frayed, and her tongue seemed thick.

"No, I would not think so. I won't keep you long from your chores."

"Come in," Peggy invited.

"No, thank you, I have to get back. I just wanted a word with you."

Peggy hesitated in her response. "All right."

"You were kind to take us in when we needed a place to stay, but now we are on our own. My child—David's child, and Sara and I want a life of peace. Your husband was generous with his land. I paid all that I could afford. Now, you seem to have made it public knowledge you are having problems in your marriage."

"You've got no right—" Peggy tried to interrupt.

Nancy raised her hand to silence her. "Oh, yes, I have a right. Don't bring me, my children, or your sister into your problems. Our character, our behavior will speak to our integrity—just as your loose talk and ugly rumors will speak to yours. Perhaps, if you sweetened your ways and stayed away from what you call 'tonic,' your husband would not find refuge in working from daylight to dark—or in a bottle, as you are suggesting to your gossiping friends."

"You've got no right—"

The door slammed in Nancy's face as she said with a sigh of satisfaction, "Have a good day, Peggy."

The tension flowed from Nancy's mind and body, as she returned home under the midday light flickering down through the canopy of leaves overhead. David so filled her mind, it seemed he had been speaking through her, and she felt whole and strong—but tired. She had been powered by the energy of her anger and resolve; now it was spent, and she longed for rest. Her feet were not only sore, but they felt as if they were sprouting roots—deep, fast penetrating roots, against which she struggled with each step. Just around the bend was home. *So far—so far.* She sopped the perspiration from her face and neck with the handkerchief. *Carol, I wish you were here—I'm so tired.* The trail began to roll beneath her feet, and she saw David in the flash of light before the darkness.

* * * * * * * * * *

Sara positioned the plates, as Carol, apron covering her hand, moved the cornbread skillet to the table. "Silas let us ride on the back of the wagon. He was going slow."

"Don't reckon that was any more dangerous than that high-flying you were doing on the swing," Carol observed.

"Josiah and I picked out the place we want to sit when school starts."

"I'm not sure you two should be sharing a table—might be too much talking going on."

"No, I want to learn—so does Josiah. We'd be quiet."

"We'll see—can you hand me that butter crock?"

Carol stopped short at the thud of horses' hooves, the clatter of spinning wagon wheels and, above the commotion, Silas's thundering, "Carol! Come quick, Carol!"

Carol rushed to throw open the door at the same time Silas mounted the porch with Nancy, like a sleeping child, in his arms.

"I found her, Carol, fainted—just up the way. Make a place for me to lay her down."

"Sara, get bedding—blankets, pillows, whatever—bring them down."

Sara was frozen, terrified.

"Move, child! Now!" Carol shook Sara's arms and turned her toward the stairs.

Silas lowered his voice, "Carol, I think her water's broken. Her dress is all wet."

"But, it's too early! It can't be!" Carol shielded her mouth with her hands. "Oh, Silas, if she loses this baby ..."

"Shush," he nodded toward Sara, a heap of quilts and pillows on legs tottering down the steps.

"Over here, Sara." In the far corner opposite the kitchen and near the fireplace, Carol made a thick pallet of pillows topped with blankets and added another pillow for Nancy's head. "Put her down here, Silas. Sara, get me some cold water in a cup and a clean dish rag."

Carol had removed Nancy's boots and had unbuttoned the high bodice of her shirtwaist, when Sara returned. Carol dampened the cloth and wiped Nancy's face, until Nancy roused and tried to speak. "Nancy, here, drink some water. You fainted."

"Carol? I was so tired—and David…" Nancy's eyes were white pools of fear, as the pain of a contraction interrupted her speech. When her breath returned, she shrieked, "No, dear God, no!" Gripping Carol's arm and sobbing, she struggled to pull herself up and begged, "No—not now—it's too soon—not the baby!"

Sara raced to Silas and hid her face against his trousers.

"Silas, take Sara out for a minute. I'm going to get these clothes off her. I'll call you when I'm done."

Carol freed her arm from Nancy's grasp and pressed Nancy back on the pillow. Holding Nancy's shoulder with one hand and her face with the other, Carol demanded, "Look at me, Nancy!" Carol waited until Nancy's shuddering ceased and her eyes focused. "Nancy, the baby is coming. You must try to help me. You have the knowledge of such things. We have not come this far to lose hope. You pray to David's God—he will give an answer. But, then, you must think, you must work—you must have courage. That's the Nancy I know—that's the Nancy David knows."

Nancy's face relaxed, as she bit her lip and fought to bring her breathing under control.

"Now, that's better. Sara is frightened by your fear. She also needs you to be strong." Carol removed Nancy's dress, petticoat, and stockings, leaving only her under slip. She cleaned Nancy's face where it had lain in the dirt and leaves of the trail. She took the pins from Nancy's loosened bun and smoothed back the hair that clung to her cheeks. She covered her with a muslin sheet.

Nancy caught Carol's arm. "Call Sara to me," she panted through clenched teeth.

* * * * * * * * *

Silas set the weeping child next to him on the step and enveloped her with his arms. Neither spoke until Sara dared to raise her head from under his wing to ask, "Is Nancy going to die?"

Silas looked at the child, then responded, "I don't think so— I hope not. Sometimes it happens that way, but not likely."

"My mother died."

"I know, Sara." Silas seemed to search for words in the clouds. "It's too bad she cannot see what a fine young woman you are today. But if you can't have your own mother, seems Nancy's sure the next best. And you've got Carol, too." Silas winked at her. "When you're a bit older and wanting to go your own way, you'll likely think you got too many mothers!" He made her smile.

"I was afraid until Nancy found me. I'm not afraid much anymore."

"No, lass, I don't expect you are." They were silent for a moment, and then Silas added, "I expect Nancy's the one's afraid now—first time mothers usually are. I think she'll be needing you to help her through her fear."

The door opened. "Sara, Nancy wants to see you. Silas, you can come in, too."

Carol held the door for Sara to enter and touched Silas's arm to stop him. "She just had another contraction. The baby is coming, but she says it could be hours. Can you take Sara home with you for the night?"

"Sure. I'll see Nancy and then go on. Josiah was with me when I found her, and I told him to run on home so I could bring her back. He was one scared rabbit. Having Sara there will be good for both of them." He guided Carol ahead of him in the door, as he added, "Likely Peggy's all stirred up wondering what's going on."

Nancy was giving Sara instructions. "...and the baby blanket—put it with the other things." Nancy took Sara's hand. "Thank you, Sara. I don't know how I could do without you. Remember, this is my first baby, but you are my first child, and I love you." Sara touched Nancy's face and then ran to accomplish her assigned tasks.

Carol called to her, "You're spending the night with the McKinnons, Sara—gather up what you need."

Nancy looked at the trembling giant towering above her. "Silas, thank you for helping me."

109

"Not to mention it, lass. I'll pray all goes with you and the baby."

"Yes, well, that's all we can do," she conceded.

"Silas is taking Sara home with him tonight, Nancy," Carol informed her.

Nancy seemed to digest the information, before commenting, "That's probably best. Silas, please keep her near where you can hear her. She may wake up frightened."

"She'll be fine, don't you worry," he assured her.

Sara returned with all the items Nancy had listed. "Everything's here."

"Thank you, Sara. You have a good time with Josiah. Go on now, with Silas—go on," she urged.

Silas took the child's hand and drew her away. Sara's gaze held Nancy's until the door came between them.

Carol placed the cold compress on Nancy's forehead, as she buckled under the contraction she had resisted until the child was out of sight. When the pain subsided, Nancy ordered, "Now, listen and remember. I must tell you what you need to know—now. I may not be able to tell you later." Carol wanted to catch the hours that flew away like birds on the wing, as she heeded, prepared, and redoubled her determination to help her friend. Together they would confront the foes of the approaching night.

* * * * * * * * *

Darkness and shadows of death. Darkness and shadows of death. The phrase whirled through her mind like dust devils stirring up leaves of suppressed memories. The wind would subside, the leaves settling for a moment, as Nancy gazed through clouds of relief to the black veil of night. To lie in David's arms just once more, to pay in agony, again—she would welcome the torment. Closing her eyes to capture the image of his face, she pressed into the gales of pain and dared them to suck her away into their swirling vortex.

The child—don't take the child. She would go with the child. *Take the child, take me. Take the child, take me!* She heard a cry— *whose voice? It is my own. Why must I shout to heaven? Do you hear me David?*

In the eye of the storm, Nancy looked out at the blazing clouds of the eastern sky. *It's coming again to toss us into the fires of heaven.*

"Nancy, the baby is coming." *I know, David. We are coming.*

Too strong—I cannot stand. Hold my hand—it is taking us away. I cannot breathe—it is sucking the life from me. Don't cry, child. Your father will come for us.

Swirling, swirling, swirling—burning, dying. The wind ceased, and Nancy fell in a heap to the ground.

"Nancy, Nancy."

Nancy awoke to Carol's soft voice. She struggled to focus on the face and the words.

111

"You've been sleeping. You were weak and tired. I let you sleep for a bit, but you must wake and suckle your daughter."

Nancy's mind was filled with the debris of the storm. She had to sweep away the refuse from her thoughts. "Daughter?" she whispered.

Tears were following the course of Carol's smile. "She is small, but she is whole." Carol turned to a second pallet at Nancy's feet and retrieved a bundle wrapped in the blanket Nancy had woven for the baby. "Margaret, this is your mother." Carol moved Nancy's arm to enfold the child laid at her side.

"She is alive? We are alive?"

"Yes, you are alive. She is alive—a scrawny little nestling, but alive and squirming."

Nancy wept, her disbelief turning to joy. "Margaret—Margaret Kaquoli." She brushed the fragile fingers across her lips, and then looked at her friend. "Thank you."

"Don't thank me—thank the One on high! I have never been so frightened!" she declared. Carol sprang to her feet. "I almost forgot—you have visitors." Carol opened the door and motioned.

Silas and Sara were devotees approaching a shrine.

Silas asked, "Are they going to be all right?"

"I think so," replied Carol. "I don't know much about childbirth, but they seem to be doing well. The baby's a wrinkled little runt with all her fingers and toes and a mop of black hair."

Nancy's laugh was weak, "I reckon I misfigured a bit. Be sure to tell Mr. Wilmouth."

Silas and Sara edged toward the bed on the floor.

"Bring a chair, Carol," Nancy directed, "so Sara can sit and hold her sister."

April 1848

Margaret swept a braid back over her shoulder, as she stood on the tips of her toes to look at the journal. A few stray hairs clung to the taffy in her other hand, and she picked them away before turning back to the record book. The delicate flourish of the scripted names and figures belied the exactitude of the register and the mundane course of business they reflected.

Terminating the sound of hooves and the snort of a horse came Carol's summons, "Margaret! Margaret Kay!"

Margaret looked at Silas and grimaced.

Silas pursed his lips and opened his eyes wide. "Better let me deal with her, Maggie." Silas rose from his stool and leaned out the opening to the saw mill office, an elevated shed with a view of the length of the operation. Ignoring the import of her tone, he extended an invitation. "Carol, Maggie's up here—come join us!"

Carol raised her skirts and marched up the three flights of stairs giving access to Margaret's lair.

Margaret peered around Silas's girth, as Carol huffed above her folded arms and declared, "I don't know which of you needs the switch more!"

"Ah, Carol, Maggie was just helping me log the day's entries. I was going to have her back in time for supper."

"Well, supper's been waiting now for over an hour. Josiah was supposed to bring Margaret back with him."

114

"Now, I told Josiah I'd bring her with me. Didn't he tell you?"

"Yes, he did, and I knew what that meant!" Carol told Margaret, "Wrap that taffy and put it away. You go wait with Old Dan while I talk to your Uncle Silas."

"But Aunt Carol," Margaret protested, "Uncle Silas will bring me home. I want to help him finish the books."

Carol raised her brows and peered askance at the child.

Margaret took Silas's hand briefly in passing and ran her palm the length of his fingers. "See you tomorrow, Uncle Silas."

"Good night, lass. May the starlight tickle your sweet dreams." he winked.

Margaret giggled and scooted away.

Carol cradled her chin in her hand and turned her head to hide the smile that crept up the corners of her mouth. When the child had descended the steps, she chided, "Silas, what are we going to do with you? You're spoiling the child. And what about Peggy? She's already in a foul temper over Josiah and Sara. You need to be getting home to her—try to keep her on an even keel."

Silas returned to the slanted worktable, replaced the pen in the ink well, and closed his register. Bitter words drifted over his shoulder. "Nothing I can do can keep her on an even keel." He shuffled papers, then said, "Come look, Carol. See what Maggie's been doing." He showed her the sheets of script, where Margaret had copied and practiced the swirls and flourishes of the ledger. He produced columns of figures and dimensions she had calculated. "She's quick, Carol! She has a real hunger to learn!"

"I know, Silas. Sometimes I think she is too hungry—for all but responsibility and self-control!" Carol shook her head in exasperation. "You and Nancy see only the eagerness and joy of the child, but she is a like a spirited filly—she needs a firm grip on a short lead."

Silas appeared whipped. "All right, Carol. You're right, as usual." He closed his log, took his hat and keys from the hook at the side of the desk, and said, "Come on, I'll give you a ride home in the wagon." Locking the door behind them, he ventured, "Maggie'd rather ride home on Dan—do you mind?"

"Not as long as she stays in sight."

* * * * * * * * *

Old Dan was tied to the newel at the bottom of the stairs. Margaret rubbed his nose and smoothed the mane on the sturdy curve of his speckled neck. A big Appaloosa, the horse had been part of her world since she could remember; he always reminded her of Uncle Silas—he was as gentle as he was strong,

Margaret loosened Dan's tether, sprang up on his saddle, and prodded him to saunter around the mill yard. Someday, she thought, she would pack a bag and ride off by herself to where the ships set sail. She would go to India and China; she would see elephants and tigers; she would smell the strange spices and exotic perfumes the explorers crossed wide oceans to possess; she would hear the clanging of temple bells calling the idolaters to worship.

Uncle Silas said she could do whatever she set her mind to do. He'd like to go with me, she thought, but he has the mills. Aunt Carol knew all about such places and things—she had taught Margaret—but, Aunt Carol would never go anywhere—she was content to read about them in books. And Mother—she had taught Margaret all about sewing, but what good were pretty clothes if there were no exciting places to wear them?

Margaret looked through the trees, across the river, and up to the mountain crests on the far side. Her father had probably hunted in those very forests. As tall and strong as Uncle Silas was, no one was taller and stronger in her dreams than David Hilderbrand.

Margaret spurred Old Dan to a gentle gallop around the perimeter of the clearing. She was the daughter of a warrior. His blood ran through her, filling every fiber of her being with courage. Margaret knew his face in her heart. She heard the rumbling of his deep voice in the night—soothing words, lulling her to sleep. His was the energy of the sun on her face, the power of the storm crashing against the mountains, the gurgling teasing of the spring as it splashed over her toes.

She climbed the mountains in search of the little people who hid in the clefts of the rocks and in the hollows of fallen logs. They knew her father—they had followed him on the hunt, they had laughed as he plunged like an otter into the icy depths of the blue hole, and they had stoked his campfire and had eased the chill of the winter snow. They could tell her tales of his daring and boldness that they alone knew—and they would tell her—she was the daughter of David Hilderbrand.

"Margaret! Slow down—poor Old Dan is working up a lather!" Aunt Carol admonished. "Come on—we're going home. You may ride ahead of the wagon, but don't go galloping off out of sight."

Margaret reined the horse to a halt and slid down his heaving side to the ground. She walked him to the watering trough, while Uncle Silas hitched the Percherons to the log wagon. Old Dan sputtered and puffed, then drank long and hard from the spring-fed tank. He was tired, Margaret knew, but she also could see the flash of fire in his eyes; within the massive heart of the old animal burned the spirit of the stallion—wild, free, and eager to run with the wind.

* * * * * * * * *

Sara covered the plates for Carol and Margaret and set them on top of the wood stove to stay warm, then rejoined Nancy and Josiah, as he was laying out paper to draw the plan for their house at Stanley.

"Has your mother come around any?" Nancy was asking.

While he spoke, Josiah took a flat pencil from his bib pocket and whittled it to a chisel point with his pocketknife. "No, she pretty much ignores me these days—like I'm not even there. Most of the time, she stays in her room. Pa says for me not to worry about it—says Sara and I got to live our own lives. I hope, when it's done, when we're married and settled, she'll get used to the idea. Me being her only child, if she expects to enjoy grandchildren, she'll have to come around."

Sara sat, chin propped in her hands, as she watched Josiah sketch the outline of their house. She liked to look at his brown hands, as they could completely enclose both of hers in their embrace; the fingers were long and flexible—artistic as they moved across the paper; and the black hair on the backs and between the joints decried anything but masculine virility. She noticed the way the hair flopped over his forehead, and she smiled as she remembered the time, she first saw him by the spring.

"Pa says we might as well make it big enough to begin with—he says he's counting on a dozen grandchildren." He looked at Sara and grinned.

She teased, "And how many wives do you plan on keeping over there, King Solomon?"

He retorted, "Just one—but she will be very, very busy!"

Sara gave his face a soft slap, as Nancy blushed with laughter.

Nancy turned serious as she stated, "I must start to work right away—twelve layettes! That will take a great deal of time! Do you think you could have them, maybe, in groups of four? That would help."

Their merriment faded with the sound of the approaching horses and wagon.

Margaret bounced into the entrance, announcing, "Josiah, I rode Dan back, but we didn't gallop. I tied him up outside." She planted a kiss on Nancy's cheek. "I'm sorry I'm late, Mama. Uncle Silas and I had to register the day's receipts." Margaret saw the floorplan lying before Josiah, and she threw her arm around his broad shoulders and asked, "Is that going to be your new house? When I come visit you at Stanley, where will I sleep?"

Sara responded, "In the woodshed if you don't learn to be on time for supper!" Sara swatted the fullness of Margaret's skirted behind.

Margaret darted behind Josiah's chair. "Ha! You missed me!"

"Margaret, wash up," her mother ordered. "Your supper is on the stove. And Aunt Carol hasn't eaten either—she had to go rounding you up."

"Have some supper with us, Uncle Silas," Margaret suggested.

"No, Maggie, I need to be getting home to Aunt Peg. We'll see you ladies later. Good evening to my clerk." He tipped his hat toward Margaret. "Josiah don't be wearin' out your welcome. Won't be that long before you and Sara'll have the rest of your years together—spare her a few nights to herself now."

"Be home soon, Pa—soon as I finish telling them about the house." Josiah's attention returned to completing the drawing.

* * * * * * * * *

Sara's face was aglow with love and admiration for the handsome young man who, with a stub of graphite, was outlining their whole life on the crinkled paper. When did they cease their childhood play and turn to see each other as man and woman? When did the loyalty and unity of best friends become the longing for union as husband and wife? Nancy remembered the exultant joy of togetherness, the wrenching pain of being apart, and the incredible wonder of newness in everything old when seen for the first time through the shared vision of love. Her heart rejoiced at their happiness, as she pushed to the recesses of her mind the ache of the loneliness to come.

But she had Margaret—she was life and joy and more than enough energy to light her days and warm her nights. Carol was concerned, she knew, for the precocious bundle of exuberance that was Nancy's daughter; but Carol was earth, and Margaret was fire and wind. Nancy was the cooling water that kept the earth from becoming parched—the firebreak between her beloved friend and the child they both adored.

A germ had taken root and was growing in Nancy's mind in recent days. She was hesitant to mention it to Carol until she weighed the merits and potential perils of her plan. The talk at the store was of the railroad's coming to Chattanooga, a more direct link between the Port of Memphis and the cotton fields of Alabama and

Georgia. The *Gazette*'s society column featured the names of well-to-dos, already circulating around the lobby of the Hotel Chattanooga—moneyed speculators with fashionable wives—women for whom quality and style, not price, determined the purchase of their apparel.

Nancy was making a good living for them in Shake Rag—her work was exceptional, prompt, and reasonable. But Nancy remembered the blue silk. More money would have come from that gown than she made in a month at Shake Rag. In Chattanooga, Margaret might have the opportunity for higher education, for a prosperous life, to make some of her fanciful daydreams come true.

But was there a place for them in a town where many of their own had been uprooted and their enemies had planted themselves? Free blacks found work there—some even attained exceptional prosperity. But with her Cherokee face, regardless of its comeliness, and with the stylish fashions her slim figure might advertise, regardless of their attractiveness, might come bitterness, hostility—the by-products of greed and guilt. She could handle herself, rise above any prejudice—but Margaret—was it fair to subject Margaret to possible mistreatment?

And Carol—what about her? Nancy would welcome her—no, long for her to come—but she knew Carol's heart was in Shake Rag, with the school—with Silas. Carol would not come. After the wedding in early October, Sara and Josiah would leave for their home over the mountain at Stanley—for their new life in a new place, which, said Silas, was just inconvenient enough for Peggy.

True, it was within walking distance—Josiah would be working the mill from there; but Sara's sweet peaceable nature would not be a daily blessing. If she took Margaret to Chattanooga, Nancy feared Carol's loneliness would be thick, smothering. Nancy determined she would give the idea more consideration before mentioning it to her.

"We'll have it finished in plenty of time to get things settled before the wedding," Josiah assured her as he folded the paper, placed it in the pocket of his overalls, and stuck the pencil behind his ear.

"Sara, Carol and I can spend a day or two helping you move and get set up. I'll even make some curtains for the windows, if you decide what you'd like."

"Oh, Nancy, you're already making my dress!" Sara protested.

"A daughter's wedding comes around only once," Nancy declared. "You are going to be a beautiful bride with nice curtains on her windows!"

As he stood to make his exit, Josiah said, "Yes, Nancy, you make sure you make nice, heavy curtains for those windows!" He winked at her and scooted toward the door, as Sara jumped up and threatened to kick his backside.

"Now, now, children," teased Carol. "Let's not do any harm to each other before the wedding!"

Josiah closed the door behind him, just in Sara's face. Sara stood with her arms folded. In a few seconds, the door eased open and Josiah peeked around it. "Good night, Nancy, Carol—good night, Maggie. Oh, yeah, good night, Sara." He wiggled his finger toward her, and Sara moved to meet his face at the aperture.

"She kissed him! She kissed him!" Margaret did a war dance around the table.

"Margaret!" Nancy laughed, "That's enough!"

Sara closed the door, then turned toward Margaret. "Little sisters should be seen and not heard."

Margaret retorted, "Well, kisses shouldn't be seen or heard!"

Carol raised her hands as if to implore for divine guidance. "What are we going to do with you, child? Are you never at a loss for words?"

"You could cut out my tongue. Mama, did you know there are places in the world where, if you tell a lie, they cut out your tongue?" Margaret stuck her tongue out and pretended to whack it. "—ike —at," she garbled.

"Margaret Kay!" said Carol.

"That's enough, Margaret," chided Nancy. "It's time for you to sit down and finish your dinner, then get ready for bed."

"—es, —a'am, I —ill." Margaret sat at her place. Retracting her tongue, she began to pick at her food. She cocked her head and announced, in her most adult voice, "I think I could still communicate reasonably well."

Sara said, "Carol, if you and Nancy don't need me, I think I'll go up and read for a while."

"Go ahead, Sara. I'll take care of our dishes. Thanks for cleaning up everything else," replied Carol.

"Tomorrow, we'll do some more fitting on your dress," suggested Nancy.

"All right," agreed Sara. "You are going to make it beautiful, I know."

"No," protested Nancy, "you, the bride, will make it beautiful."

Sara smiled and ascended the stairs to the bedrooms.

* * * * * * * * *

Sara looked around the cubicle of space she shared with Carol. She sat on her bed and picked up the book of poetry Silas had given her after he learned she and Josiah would marry. "You're already best friends," he had said, as they sat before the apple cake she had made. "You know each other like brother and sister. That's the important thing—friendship." Silas had spoken between bites of cake, and Sara had vacillated between emotional tears and giggles, as he orated and gesticulated with his fork. "But now you need to love and appreciate each other as man and woman—like those two in that book." He had pointed with his fork to the leather-bound volume she held in her hands. Then, he thrust it at the cake. "Friendship is the icing in the middle that holds the layers together;

romance is the icing on top and all around that makes it real pretty and sweet." He had licked his fork and added, "And I'll have me another piece, if you don't mind." He had slapped Josiah on the back. "Son, if she does everything else as well as she bakes apple cake, you're going to be one happy man!"

There was a far, deep place in her heart where light could not reach, where she reserved the memory of her father and the remnant of sadness she still felt for his loss. Nancy had been the only mother she had ever known, and Silas was as much a father to her as to Josiah. Sara loved Silas with a depth and warmth she could not remember feeling for her father, but there was still a sense that part of her was missing. Before the day when the soldiers came, she recalled no history of her own to tell her children; even her father's face was blurred and fading when she struggled to bring it to mind.

Rather than a link in a long chain of family, she was part of a commune consolidated by loneliness, compatibility—perhaps, even fear. And, yes, love—she loved her adopted family and felt secure and grounded in their love for her. Why, then, was there always an empty, aching spot in her heart she could not fill? She could not even explain it to Josiah and discuss it with him, she feared, lest he think himself insufficient to make her happy and whole.

And she was happy—happier than she had thought she could be. Josiah was life, light, joy, completion. When she thought of him, she longed for the days when she might be called "Mrs. McKinnon," and the nights when she might lie in the passion of his embrace and in the shelter of his arms till daybreak.

Sara would miss her family at Shake Rag, but she looked forward to making a home in Stanley for Josiah and herself, on the gentle slope of riverside land Silas had bought for them as a wedding gift. He said they needed to be on their own, yet close enough for Josiah to have some income from the mill. She knew he was concerned that Peggy, with her peaks of near-madness and valleys of melancholy, might intrude on their happiness. Even now, Josiah, like Silas, left early and returned late, to avoid his mother's alleged bouts of illness, her belittling of him, and her backhanded criticism of his wife-to-be. In Peggy's mind, Josiah was hers; and she would seek to keep him, if she had to disparage her competition or even demean the value of the prize.

Sometimes Sara felt sorry for Peggy, the axis of her own empty world—living in self-imposed emotional isolation, yet surrounded by people—people to love, if only she could, people to love her, if only enough. And she felt sorry for Silas—so many years of unhappiness. He had married the beautiful porcelain miniature— a cold, yet fragile reflection of the warmth and sturdiness that was Carol. Only Carol, it seemed, with so much love to give, had found contentment—in Nancy and her children, in the school, in Josiah— in being near the man, Sara now recognized, whom Carol loved. If they only knew the long hours Sara and Josiah talked, assessing their unusual family, wondering what forces had brought them together and had made them the people they were!

Sara laid the poetry book on the lamp table between the beds and picked up the magazine plate of the wedding dress Nancy was making. Nancy—Sara had never been able to call her mother, though Sara could not love anyone more than she loved Nancy—or Carol. Sara traced the sweep of skirt with her finger. She wondered what each of them would be like alone—Carol without Nancy, Nancy without Carol. Carol was a mill wheel and Nancy the stream that forced its turning.

Sara unbuttoned her boots and slipped them off. She fluffed up the down pillow, then lay back to cross her feet on the bed. She studied the drawing of the bride and tried to picture herself as the elegant model, swathed in tucks and lace above and below the reed-thin waist. *If the soldiers had never come, where would I be today?* she wondered. Still dressed in her day clothes, she fell asleep, holding the designer's sketch and remembering the little girl who cried for the father who never returned.

* * * * * * * * *

Nancy and Margaret had gone to their room, and Carol sat beside the last lamp to be extinguished before closing her own day. As it was most evenings, she was weary to the depth of her bones, but she needed some time for her racing mind to slow to the crawl of her body. She sat at her place at the table and watched the flame.

Each day, the stretch between wakening and bedtime seemed to grow longer, yet the days were flying away faster than she could catch them and savor their richness. As much as she loved those she called family, as satisfied as she was with her teaching, at moments like this, she reminisced about Kaquoli and missed the quiet, confident, contemplative nature that characterized the person she once was.

She had said, *Love is always something to be given*—and she had given and had been rewarded in return—her life was full and happy at times. But contentment—was there contentment? A part of her wanted to gallop away with Maggie's same exuberant abandon. Another part wanted to be like Nancy, to hold up a fine dress and say, *See, this is what I have made with my own hands!*

Carol studied her hands. They were sturdy with long fingers, some of which crooked a bit, and the skin on the backs was etched with fine, leathery lines portending old age. What had she accomplished in over forty years? Being midwife at Maggie's birth was the nearest to anything of lasting value, and to that experience she was only a conscripted bystander. She would never give birth to her own child. She would never be able to look into the face of her son or daughter to say: *You are mine—begotten of love and born of me.* Even her teaching, which brought her such pleasure, was for the edification of her students and, thereby, the accreditation of their parents. Perhaps, one day, a man of renown would think back to the schoolhouse, where "Miss Carol" had uttered influential words that charted his course of greatness; and he would say: *Had it not been for my teacher, I would not be the man I am today.*

Carol smiled and shook her head. She knew she had been feeling sorry for herself since Sara and Josiah had decided to marry and to move to Stanley. Nancy had Margaret, Sara had Josiah—even in their misery, Peggy had Silas. As important as she knew she was to all of them, Carol belonged to only herself—and she felt she had lost even herself somewhere up on the mountain overlooking Shake Rag.

Carol followed the flame of her lamp upstairs to find Sara asleep on top of the covers, the picture of the bridal gown still held in her hand. Carol slipped it from her grasp and laid it on the trunk under the window. She set the lamp on the table, moved the blanket from under Sara's feet, and covered the girl without disturbing her to undress.

Carol prepared herself for bed, then moved the curtains aside to allow more breeze through the screened window. The moon and stars were bright in the night sky; and, in the distance, she could see the schoolhouse—tranquil, idyllic, framed in the light of evening. Silas had maintained the building well all these years, even adding a bell tower when the town leaders decided to invite a preaching student to come down from Chattanooga to hold regular Sunday services.

She must remember this scene and describe it to her students. During the school term, weather permitting, one afternoon a week, Carol took her students on a nature walk to sketch something of beauty in their environment. That might range from the vibrant spot of a ladybug on a single tuft of grass, to the blue of winter mountains with clouds encircling their heads like smoke rings, to the studious face of a friend in deep concentration on his own sketch.

Along with other principles suggested by herself or the students, "Look for beauty" was one of the "Good Living Guidelines" she had posted on the wall at the front of the classroom. Not the traditional schoolroom roster of rules, the Guidelines was composed of ideas inspected, discussed, and included only after unanimous agreement. *Look for beauty.* Carol had not been looking for it, but it was there—in the pristine white structure of man's making, in the hazy moonlight of heaven, and in the spire that bound the one to the other in the quiet stillness of the night.

Carol started to turn toward her bed, when movement in the schoolyard caught her eye. Had she seen something, she wondered, or had a cloud crossed the moon to cast a darting shadow? Carol focused her eyes and strained her vision. There, again! There was something moving from the far side of the building, into the light of the schoolyard, then around the other side. She waited and watched, but there was no other sign of motion. Wait! Was that a flicker of light at the window? Yes! What could that—

"Fire!" she screamed. "Nancy, fire at the school building!"

Clad only in her nightdress, Carol bolted down the stairs, threw open the door, and raced toward the schoolyard. Terror stilled her mind but energized her feet. As she approached the schoolhouse, she saw flames licking the windows to the right of the door. Hearing feet behind her, she turned to see Nancy, followed by Sara and

Margaret, running toward her. "I'll sound the bell and do what I can. You all get Silas and Josiah."

"I'll help Carol!" Nancy yelled to the girls. "You go on!"

With Nancy close behind, Carol tore up the steps and into the building. "Ring the bell, Nancy!" she ordered.

The steeple bell began clanging, as Carol grabbed a rug from inside the door and began beating the blaze that was spreading from the floor, up to the window, and across to the corner of the structure.

"Nancy, get the bucket in the store room and start bringing water from the faucet!" Carol played the fire's cruel, deceptive game—crushing a flame in one spot, only to have it spring up in another. She ignored the smoke stinging her eyes and choking her breath.

"Here, Carol! Take this! I'm filling the waste can!"

Carol took the bucket and splashed it against the slender fingers of fire tickling the corner. Picking up the rug, she again attacked the voracious enemy, so determined to ravage her property and plunder her work and dreams.

Nancy returned dragging the second container. "Help me with this, Carol!"

Dropping the rug, Carol took one side of the trashcan, and, together, they swung the vessel upward, drenching the floor and part of the window.

"More water! We've got to keep it contained until help comes!" Tears and perspiration were streaking the soot on Carol's face, as she spoke to the fire, "You won't get the books and the maps."

It seemed Carol, Nancy, and the fire made time stand still.

Nancy was returning with more water, when Silas dashed into the room and grabbed Carol's wrist. "Give me that rug! Get out whatever you can—out the back—just in case!" Josiah came behind his father with a bucket in each hand. "Josiah, tell the girls to go around back—help Carol and Nancy take things out!"

Josiah returned with two more filled buckets, but cried, "Pa, there's smoke coming from the roof outside! It must be in the walls!"

"Help Carol get the maps down, Josiah!"

"Silas, we've got men and buckets!" shouted the voice of Lester Wilmouth, as he skidded to a stop inside the door.

"Get a brigade going in here. When I get up on the roof, you all start a line to me up there." Silas dashed outside.

Carol and Josiah dismounted the maps and carried them outside to the playground, where piles of books were scattered, and a disorganized assemblage of desks and seats was growing. On their return, they crossed paths with Nancy, who was bringing a box of paints and brushes from the storeroom.

"Nancy don't go back," Carol ordered. "We'll make one last check and then leave it to the men."

The sound of crashing timbers brought them to a halt. A plume of flame shot from the roof.

"Pa!" Josiah screamed. "Pa was on the roof!" He plunged through the storeroom door into the midst of timbers, like giant broken, blazing matchsticks.

"Pa! Pa!"

"Silas!" Carol's voice screamed into the haze of smoke.

"Over here, Carol! Help me!"

Carol followed the sound of Josiah's call. Silas was alive but moaning and trapped beneath a fallen timber.

"I'll have to lift this. Can you pull him out?"

Carol nodded and crooked her hands under Silas's armpits.

Josiah's face contorted with effort, then he said, "Pull!"

Carol struggled, moving him only by inches.

"Pull! I can't hold it much longer!"

A surge flowed down her long, narrow back, giving Carol the strength of a cart ox. She pulled the big Scot across the floor to the storeroom, as Josiah released the timber to go crunching through the plank flooring. He joined Carol, and, together, they dragged Silas to the safety of the playground.

In the stillness of midnight, moon glow, a few oil lamps, and the shell of the schoolhouse lighted the faces of the community as they hovered around Silas McKinnon, his son, and the woman who knelt on the ground at Silas's head and held his singed face in her hands. Weariness and concern for the man they all loved and respected denied them any satisfaction in knowing they had saved a good part of the building.

Nancy ripped the ruffle from the bottom of her nightdress, soaked it in cold water, and washed the soot from Silas's face.

Josiah and Sara, holding hands, knelt beside Silas, while Margaret, her eyes locked on his face, stood at his feet.

The world was quiet, save for the sounds of crackling embers, coughs, and the chirping of night creatures coming out of hiding.

Josiah ventured the question: "Nancy, is he all right?"

"I don't know," she replied. "He's alive. He's not bleeding that I can see." Nancy sat back on her haunches and looked at Carol, smoothing the hair on Silas's temples, brushing her fingers through the whiskers on his face. Nancy saw Carol was wearing her love for the entire world to see. Then, she remembered, scanned the crowd, and wondered; *Where is Peggy?*

"Nancy, look!" Carol whispered.

Silas had opened his eyes and was looking around at the faces peering down on him. A smile seemed to be interrupted by a fit of coughing which racked his body until he was speechless. He gasped, "I like being the center of attention."

Nancy and Carol laughed through their tears, and Carol leaned down to kiss his forehead.

"Send them all home," he whispered to Carol.

"What?" she asked, leaning closer.

He panted, "Tell them to go home. Get some rest."

Carol announced, "He says you all go on home now. Get some rest. We'll see to him. Thank you."

Nancy rose to her feet to extend her thanks and to assure their neighbors they could handle things.

Carol called out, "Thank you. We'll get the school rebuilt before you know it—we'll be ready come fall."

"You sure I can't stay to help?" asked Lester.

Silas rocked his head and raised an arm to wave in response.

As his earnest dark eyes sought Silas's, Wilmouth grasped the extended hand and enclosed it within his own. "You say the word, and we'll start rebuilding. I'm here whenever you need me." He wiped his brow with his sleeve, replaced his hat, and nodded farewell.

They all watched as their friends and neighbors, tired yet content, turned toward their homes to rest before the new day.

Then their eyes returned to Silas McKinnon.

"They're gone, Pa. Are you ready to go home?" asked Josiah.

Tears streamed from Silas's eyes and made a network of veins in the soot on his face. "I reckon I am, son. But I can't walk."

"We'll help you, Pa. Carol and I got you out of there." Josiah moved but was stopped by Silas's hand on his arm.

"No, son. I mean I can't walk. I can't move my legs."

* * * * * * * * *

In the stillness of the early morning hours, a quiet procession trod the trail toward the McKinnon home place. Margaret drooped

136

astride one horse, led by Nancy. Sara followed, and Josiah led another horse pulling the drag litter that carried Silas McKinnon. Carol walked by his side and held his hand.

Leaving Margaret with Sara at Nancy's house, the remainder of the party trudged on toward the McKinnons'. The windows were black and lifeless, as the group turned the fence corner toward their destination, and Carol wondered if Peggy was in one of her tonic-induced oblivions. She hoped so, as this was no time for either Peggy's hysteria or her histrionics.

Josiah preceded them to light the lamps for their path into the house. Then he returned to release the litter from the horse and lowered Silas to the ground. Nancy took the end of a pole at Silas's head and Carol the pole end opposite; Josiah seized the ends of both poles at Silas's feet. In unison, they lifted his heavy frame and carried him into the bedroom, where Josiah lowered the end of the litter and, with the remaining strength of his father's arms to assist him, eased Silas onto the bed.

As the women stood beside them, Josiah began removing Silas's boots. Studying his father's face, Josiah said, "Tell me if I hurt you, Pa."

Silas's reply was soft. "Son, I wish you were causing me agony, but there's none—I don't feel a thing."

Josiah directed his words to Carol. "Maybe you better find Ma and tell her to come—if you can wake her up. I'll help Pa get cleaned up, so he can rest."

Carol gestured to Nancy and said, "Come with me."

137

The women searched the house, porches, and outbuildings; Peggy was nowhere to be found.

On their way back to the bedroom, in the parlor, Carol caught Nancy's arm and spoke in a subdued voice, "I don't think we'll find her anytime soon."

"Why would you say that? Where would she be?"

"Just before I saw the fire, I saw something—or someone— moving around the schoolhouse. I think the fire was set, and, most likely, it was Peggy that started it."

"Carol! You think Peggy would do something like that?"

"I think Peggy would do anything with enough tonic in her! And where was she? There's a fire, the alarm sounds, the town turns out—where's Peggy? If she were just indisposed—as usual, she'd be passed out around here somewhere."

"Where would she go?"

"I don't know." Carol's voice broke with emotion, as she shook her finger and vowed, "But, I swear, Nancy, if she comes back, I may kill her."

Carol's shoulders were shaking, as Nancy gathered her into her arms.

Nancy suppressed the anger boiling in her gut and clasped her friend to her breast. Choking on her own words, she declared, "Don't say that, Carol! You don't mean that!"

Carol wept. Then, avoiding Nancy's eyes, she raised her head and wiped the tears from her face. "Oh, the sentiment is real enough—but, no, I could never hurt her." Smoothing her hair back from her face, she looked at Nancy, then smiled. "I'd let you do it."

Nancy sniffled and rubbed her arm across her eyes and nose. "As you said, 'The sentiment is real.'" She noticed the sleeves of her nightdress were damp, dirty, and streaked with soot. "Let's make sure Silas and Josiah are settled and, then, go home. It'll be daylight before long, and we'll come back."

Josiah, his elbow on the night table, his forehead propped on his hand, was sitting in a chair beside the bed, where Silas lay covered with a sheet showing only his flushed face, with his graying auburn beard and wreath of hair. The lamp was turned low, and Silas appeared to be resting.

Nancy whispered, "We couldn't find Peggy anywhere."

Josiah's eyelids dropped as he sighed. "I'll deal with her tomorrow."

Carol asked, "How is he?"

Josiah raised his head and thought before speaking. "Covered with bruises, especially across his legs where the board fell. But he's not bleeding—at least not on the outside. No swelling yet, no parts like broken bones sticking out." Josiah rubbed his eyes, then stood and whirled toward the parlor.

Carol ran after him, while Nancy stood at the door and followed them with her eyes.

"Josiah, stop!" Carol called.

Josiah sat in his father's chair and pressed the heels of his hands against his eyelids.

Carol knelt in front of him and held his arms until he was ready to speak.

"Aunt Carol, his back is broken—I know it is. And if it is, he ain't going to walk again—never!"

"Now, Josiah, we don't know that—not yet! The doctor'll be making his rounds through here soon. He'll tell us. We just have to hope and pray!" Carol held Josiah's face in her hands until she had his gaze and calmed him. "Josiah, even if he can't walk again, he is still alive. He's still Silas. We can give him whatever help he needs and wants—and just be glad he's alive!"

* * * * * * * * *

The water lapped around the boulders, tumbled out into the river like giant steppingstones. Margaret and Sara perched on a rock in the shade of the branches overhanging the banks and dangled their bare feet in the cool ripples of current.

Margaret was still tired. Nothing as momentous as the events of the preceding night had ever happened in her life. The excitement of the fire and the shock and anxiety over Silas had delayed her sleep; the ensuing nightmares had defeated her rest.

"Sara, is Uncle Silas going to die?" Margaret's new voice was gentle and soft.

She noticed Sara's eyes were still swollen from crying.

"No, Margaret—he's not going to die." Sara looked across the river at the lush green of the mountains set against the blue sky.

"When can I see him?"

"Later today. We'll take supper to them."

Margaret did not argue. "Let's walk up the bank to the schoolyard. I want to see what it looks like today. Maybe pick some honeysuckle from the vines near the spring."

Sara was numb—weariness and worry had sapped her energy. She had been awake all night, it seemed; troubling memories of the fire and the collapsing roof had become terrifying nightmares that had awakened her. A whirling cycle of the conscious and unconscious had blurred the distinction between waking and sleep, leaving her head and body aching and her mind in a fog.

"All right," Sara agreed as she picked up her boots. "But we have to keep a safe distance. You can't go in."

Part of Sara longed to be with Josiah as he watched over Silas, but she could not help either of them, and Silas needed his son's undivided attention. Nancy and Carol were depending on her to help Margaret, as the events of the preceding evening had been traumatic, smashing the child's exuberant spirit like a kite in a downdraft.

Last night Sara had washed and was waiting in her bedclothes by the cold fireplace downstairs, when Nancy and Carol had returned from the McKinnons'. The lamp on the stand next to her had shed sufficient light for reading, but the words on the page had been only meaningless exercise for her eyes. When she had tried to sleep later in the early morning hours, her mind was still racing, and her head swollen from the expenditure of weeping. Silas was more than his protective size and strength, more than the massive, enveloping arms that had comforted her since childhood. He was love and kindness and humor—all the nourishment her hungry soul craved as the frightened child she had been, all the qualities on which she flourished now as a woman in love with the son cast in his image. But Silas—how could Silas find any joy in life as half a man? She prayed for his healing—but, if not that, for an answer.

Margaret carried her shoes in one hand and trailed a stick behind her as they strolled along the bank. Only since Sara had suggested they go outside for a walk, had Margaret even initiated conversation. Sara thought she needed reassurance by seeing Silas, but, first, it needed to be determined how Silas would react to Maggie's seeing him. Theirs was a special relationship—Silas was Margaret's father, mentor and best friend, all in the guise of a big, soft bear, whose gentle arms had rocked her as an infant, cradled her as a sleeping child, and still swung her up to the tree tops in gales of delight.

Margaret continued toward the creek that flowed between the house and the school building, as Sara stopped at the bend of the river to watch the Massengill boys trolling close to the bank. How strange it seemed that, after the tumult of the early morning hours, life could appear so placid and mundane. Somehow, it was comforting to watch the skiff gliding in the still water near the river's edge, relaxing to hear the soft plop of the baited hook as it hit the surface. Sara felt she might curl up in the tall grass and be lulled to sleep in this very spot.

The lightning bolt of a scream shattered the tranquil moment and seared a direct hit on Sara's heart. She raced toward Margaret's shrieks that came without stopping—again and again, as if strips of flesh were being torn from her insides. Sara was eased to see that Margaret was standing at the edge of the creek, but she reached her to find she was ashen and immobile, save for the siren issuing from the depths of her being.

Sara stooped to take Margaret's arms. Shaking her to halt the wails and to draw her attention, she demanded, "Margaret, what's wrong!" Following the gaze of the frozen child, Sara gasped. Pulling Margaret into her bosom to shield her, she turned them both away from the horror lying among the cascading rocks and falls of the spring.

* * * * * * * * * *

Josiah was asleep in the other bedroom, and Carol sat next to Silas, her head resting on the cover atop her folded arms. Silas's mild, sputtering snore was lulling Nancy to sleep at her own bedside station, where she had sat finishing the tucks on a lace-trimmed camisole for Sara's trousseau. She lay the garment aside—twice she had pricked her finger as her eyes failed to focus.

The sound of feet stumbling up the porch steps drew Nancy into the parlor. She reached the door and opened it just as Sara's arm stretched toward the handle. With the other arm, Sara supported Margaret, who wore the face of death.

"Come out!" Sara wheezed and tugged on Nancy's arm.

"Sara, what's wrong?" She felt Margaret's face. "Margaret? What's happened?"

Sara shivered, and her voice trembled, "Peg—Peggy—she's dead—in the spring."

"Oh, dear Lord!" Nancy exclaimed.

"Margaret found her." Sara's trembling was exaggerated by Margaret's stillness.

"Come into the dining room," Nancy ordered. She pulled two chairs together and seated the girls. Retrieving shawls from the hall tree, she instructed Sara to "Hold her," and covered them, adding, "I'll make some tea." Sara cuddled her sister in her arms.

Nancy was startled by the appearance of Carol at the doorway. Her voice was calm as she asked, "Nancy, what has happened?"

Nancy squared her shoulders and replied, "Carol, it's Peggy. Her body is in our creek, near the mouth of the river. Margaret found her."

Carol dropped her head into her hands. "Dear God, please— not this, too!"

Nancy went to Carol and laid her hand on her friend's arm. "Do you want me to tell Josiah?"

Carol had thought she had spent all the tears in her reserve, but fresh ones followed in their course. "No, I'll tell him. Go ahead and see to the girls."

Carol padded across the room where Silas lay and entered the back bedroom, where Josiah, one arm covering his eyes, was sprawled asleep on the bed. He had removed his shoes and shirt but was clad in his undershirt and suspendered trousers. She moved the arm from his eyes. "Josiah, wake up!" she whispered. "Wake up!"

Josiah opened his eyes and focused them on the woeful face above him. Awakened by realization and remembrance, he inquired, "Pa—is he all right?"

"Yes," Carol replied. "Get up. Come with me."

Josiah pulled on his boots and picked up his shirt, as he followed Carol. He noticed his father was still snoring as he passed through the house to the front porch.

"Where are we going?"

Carol stopped and turned toward her nephew as they descended the steps. She seized his eyes and spoke, "Josiah, your mother is dead. Margaret and Sara saw her body in the creek between here and the schoolhouse."

When the words gained access to Josiah's understanding, he whirled and ran toward the spring feeding into the river. Dreading the scene before her, Carol hastened to catch up.

Josiah sat on a rock in the spring, the water splashing over his feet, as if it were asking to play. He cradled his mother in his arms, as if she were a rag doll, fallen by chance from the arms of the child, amusing himself in the shallows.

Carol gathered up her skirt and waded into the creek. She bent in front of Josiah and placed her arms under the lifeless form. "Josiah, help me get her home."

Josiah looked at Carol, then at his mother. Together, they lifted Peggy and, making their way around stones and kneeholes, carried her the quarter mile to the house.

Nancy left the girls with their tea and returned to wait at Silas's bedside. As she entered the room, she found him awake and pushing himself up with his arms to lean against the headboard.

"Here, Silas, let me get these pillows behind you," Nancy offered.

Silas was flushed and sputtering with frustration, as he pulled against the heaviness of his lower body. "Worthless! Absolutely worthless!" He collapsed against the cushions behind his head and shoulders. He turned away from Nancy. "Where's Josiah?"

"He'll be back soon." Nancy busied herself bustling about the room, straightening here and there.

"Carol?" he asked.

"She's with Josiah. They won't be gone long."

He thought aloud, "I'm supposed to be at the mill. The men will wonder where I am. I need Josiah to take over for me."

Nancy tried to reassure him. "The men know what you went through battling the fire this morning. They'll assume you're getting some rest."

Silas heaved a heavy sigh that culminated in a racking cough.

Nancy said, "I'll get you some water."

As she entered the hall, she heard feet and movement on the porch, and the door opened.

Sodden from the knees down, Carol entered and closed the door behind her, whispering, "Nancy, we need a blanket from the chest at the foot of Silas's bed."

Nancy nodded and retraced her steps to the bedroom.

"Who's that?" Silas asked.

"Josiah and Carol are back—they'll be right in." She retrieved a blanket and scurried out before Silas could ask more questions.

Carol took the blanket and went out to the porch. In a few moments, she returned, followed by Josiah.

Sara left her shawl around Margaret and went to the door of the dining room to watch. She was unsure how Josiah would be, what he would expect of her, how she should act, what she should say. Death had touched her life, but never in her remembrance, never in the life of one she loved as she loved Josiah—and never so near and vivid as the body in the spring.

Josiah followed Carol into the hallway. He looked at Nancy, then sought Sara's eyes.

The expression on Josiah's face was new to her, and she was frightened by the intensity of grief it revealed. She walked a few steps toward Josiah, who spanned the remaining distance between them in a heartbeat and hugged her as if she were life itself.

Standing at Silas's bedside, Sara willed her love and strength into Josiah, as he grasped her hand and sought to be the man his father needed him to be—groped for the right words to tell his father what he needed to know.

Silas had turned toward the couple as they had entered the room. He had studied Josiah—a long, searching gaze, before he had asked, "Where you been, son?"

Josiah squeezed Sara's hand to the point of pain as he spoke, "Pa, Ma's dead."

Silas frowned, wincing. He allowed the words to penetrate his understanding. He whispered, "Peg? Dead?"

Josiah closed his eyes, nodded, and sucked a deep breath before continuing, "Sara and Margaret were out walking. Margaret found her in the spring this side of the school building. Looked to me like she might have lost her footing crossing the creek and hit her head—knocked her out and she rolled down where it was deep enough to drown her—not more than a few inches where her face was."

Silas looked up at the ceiling as tears rolled down his cheeks and onto the pillows. He exhaled, sighing, "Ah, Peggy, Peggy!"

They all remained silent, until Silas turned to them and asked, "You say Maggie found her?"

Sara nodded, and Josiah replied, "Yes, sir."

"How is she?"

Josiah looked at Sara, who replied, "Not good, Uncle Silas. She was terrified—just kept screaming. She hasn't said a word since."

Silas closed his eyes. The quiet was smothering—then Silas said, "Bring her to me."

Nancy and Carol were sitting in the parlor as Sara went to fetch the child. She paused and spoke to them in passing, "He wants to see Maggie."

Nancy nodded, and Carol said, "Maybe it will help them both."

Margaret still sat huddled under the shawls and stared at the black pit of the fireplace.

"Margaret?" Sara approached her, but Margaret remained motionless. "Margaret, Uncle Silas wants to see you." Margaret looked at Sara. "Uncle Silas is asking for you to come see him."

Margaret stood, gathered the wraps around her, and accompanied Sara to the place Silas lay.

Margaret tried so hard to think, but her mind seemed to be stuck. She understood what people were saying, but they were words without feelings, without questions. *Go, Margaret. Sit here, Margaret. Drink this, Margaret. You're cold, Margaret.* She could not find the words to respond or to ask why. She only envisioned the place of death, filled with the sweet fragrance of honeysuckle—and the body—twisted, grotesque, in the gurgling fall of water. One arm was wedged between the rocks; the other bobbed as a cascade fell into the pool where it lay. The hair had come loose from its pinning, and tendrils floated, streaming through the current like riverweed.

Sara guided Margaret to the door of the bedroom, where the child stopped and observed the man lying on the bed under the sheet with his back propped against the headboard. Casting a troubled glance toward Margaret and caressing Sara's face as he passed, Josiah left the room so they could be alone with Silas.

"Maggie, lass, I'm glad you've come to see me." Silas smiled, but the child stood still. "Please, Maggie, come here." He held out his hand.

Sara nudged Maggie's shoulder and said, "Go on, Maggie. Uncle Silas needs you."

Uncle Silas needs you. The words touched a chord of awareness. The body in the creek—Margaret jerked and blinked away from the picture that slammed against her eyelids and shot a pain through her head—it was Peggy, Uncle Silas's wife.

Margaret crept toward the bed beckoned by the outstretched hand.

"Will you crawl up here next to me, Maggie? I'm scared and cold."

Maggie saw the tears in Silas's eyes, as Sara helped her up on the high bed.

The child nestled in the cradle of Silas's arm. "That's it, Maggie." He smoothed her hair. "I feel better already. We've had a hard time, haven't we, lass?"

Sara, sitting at their side, noticed her sister's head nod against Silas's chest, and she covered her mouth with her hand to restrain a sob. Silas looked to the ceiling and struggled to control his voice. "But it's so much better now that you're here—and Sara's here."

Sara placed her arm over Margaret and rested her hand on Silas's chest.

"As bad as things can be sometimes, we have each other, and we can help each other get through them." Silas stroked Sara's hand. "I'm sorry you two had to see Aunt Peg the way she was today. We all have to die sometime, but accidents like that are terrible. I hope you both can put it far away in your minds where it won't hurt you too much."

Margaret pressed her face into Silas's chest and wept.

A few minutes had passed, when Margaret wiped her nose on her sleeve and asked, "Are you going to die, too, Uncle Silas?"

Silas thought for a moment. "Oh, sure, I'll die someday—we all have to die someday. But I'll try to stay healthy and be careful— and you do the same, and we'll all be together as long as we can. All right?"

"All right," Maggie agreed, her face sad but accepting.

"Now, Maggie, it seems I do have a problem I need your help with," Silas ventured.

Maggie tilted her chin up to look at him. "What is it?"

"Well, you see me laid up here in this bed, don't you?"

Maggie nodded. "You got hurt in the fire."

"Yep, it seems I did. Well, right now my legs aren't working."

"What's wrong with them?"

"Not sure, Maggie. They just won't move when my head tells them to move. I'm going to need your help for a while—maybe help me with some paperwork, figures—like you usually do, but maybe just let me borrow your legs some, too."

Maggie cuddled against him and ran her fingers through his beard. "Sure, Uncle Silas."

"Well, can you tell me one thing first?"

Maggie looked up to see a tear running into the corner of his smile.

"Can you tell me if your legs will hold up a man my size without crumpling?"

* * * * * * * * *

As she had for weeks now, Carol made her regular afternoon trek to take food, but she was never sure how she would find Silas. He had been biding his time as he could—reading, looking over reports from the mills. But, Josiah said, it seemed his father was sleeping later each morning and dousing the light earlier each evening. He had seemed, at best, contemplative in recent days, and Carol feared melancholia might kill his ebullient spirit.

She shifted the heavy basket to one hand, knocked, then waited. After a few moments, she heard Josiah's boots clunking through the hall to open the door.

Retrieving the container, Josiah said, "Come on in, Aunt Carol."

"Is he decent?"

"Well, he's dressed and ready for company, if that's what you mean," Josiah grinned, as he carried the basket toward the kitchen. He lifted the towel covering. "What have you got in here— are we having a party or something? If you keep feeding Pa like this, he's going to be fat as a hog!"

"I heard that, son!" Silas's voice called out from the bedroom. "Carol's got a real gift for cooking," His voice grew louder, as he appeared in the parlor in a rolling chair, "and I aim to appreciate that gift."

"Silas! Look at you! What is this? It's wonderful!" Carol rushed to admire the new conveyance.

"My men made it for me—the finest wheeled chair to be had! So, see, I've got to keep up my strength to propel myself along."

Josiah returned from the kitchen, admonishing, "That's right, Pa, but the more of you there is to maneuver, the harder it's going to be."

Silas patted the girth resting on his lifeless legs. "Now that I'm up and going, all that food won't be settling around here. And I aim to be getting back to work as I can—with Josiah's help, of course."

"Well, I think this is all just really fine!" Carol declared. "And it's good to hear you sounding so much better, Silas—"

Josiah interrupted, "Aunt Carol, would you mind staying with Pa a while and fixing his food for him? I promised Sara I'd come by before dinner to talk about the wedding plans and stay to eat with her."

"Why, surely—but she didn't say anything about it—hope I haven't carted off too much with me."

"Don't worry. Maybe you'd like to eat with Pa this evening—that way he won't be alone." Josiah took his hat from the hall tree and trotted out the door.

Silas called after him, "With Sara's cooking, you'll be looking like your old Pa before long!"

Their laughter died, and Carol said, "Well, I'd better get that food laid out. Guess you'll be having dinner in the dining room tonight." She started toward the kitchen.

"Come, Carol, sit down a bit."

"But—"

"No—no buts, sit." He patted the chair beside him.

Carol moved to sit stiffly on the edge of the seat. She could not remember the last time she had made conversation with Silas alone, without the buffer of family or work. Even after all the years, even though his hefty frame was confined to a wheelchair, his proximity still made her breathless and uneasy. She smoothed a stray hair back into place.

"Carol..." He cleared his throat. "Carol, you—and Sara, have taken mighty good care of us since Peg died, and I want to thank you."

"Oh, Silas, we're family—that's what family does."

"I know, I know—but you have been the glue of this family since you came back—don't think I don't know that. You held us together when Peg herself was falling apart—and likely the family with her, had it not been for you—and all without a word of complaint."

Discomfort sat between them like a third person.

"Silas, you are my family. I did only what was best for my family."

Silas searched his folded hands for any words they might hold. "We should have been your family—Josiah and me, and would have been, if not for my foolishness."

"Silas." Carol stood to leave.

"Sit—please, Carol."

Misty blue eyes forced her back to her seat.

"All those many years ago, I made a terrible mistake."

"Silas, Peggy was my sister—"

"Yes, and we both loved her—as much as any people could love Peg. Perhaps—perhaps, she wouldn't have been as bad off as she was, if not for me."

"Silas, there was something not right about Peg. I don't think anyone was responsible."

"Maybe, maybe not—but I always sensed she knew I married the wrong sister, and, over time, it just ate her up."

"Silas, I can't listen to this—" Carol stood.

Silas's grip on her wrist was an iron clamp. "But you must! I cannot go on denying my feelings for you. What are your feelings for me?"

"You are my sister's husband," Carol protested.

"No, I was your sister's husband—and now I am only half a man—"

"Don't say that, Silas."

"But it's true. I have come to terms with it. What are your feelings for me—now?"

Carol collapsed into the chair. So many years she had dreamed of a day when the veil might be lifted from her heart—now the time had come, and she was frightened. More than the day the soldiers came, more than the stockade, more than their escape, more than Sara's birth, more than the fire—the baring of her soul to the only man she had ever loved terrified her.

"I love you, Silas." The sound of her own voice surprised her. She looked at him. "I love you, Silas. I always have, and I always will." Carol felt lighter, freer, than she had since the day she learned Silas would marry Peggy. She had never realized the oppressive weight she had carried, and now she wanted to fly away singing into the clouds.

156

"Even now? What's left of me?"

"Even now," she laughed through tears of relief, "and it seems to me that's a pretty substantial portion!"

Silas wept.

"Silas, please, don't." Carol knelt in front of him and held his hands.

"I'm sorry, Carol—I want to ask you to marry me. I want to open my eyes to your face in the morning and to kiss you before dousing the light at night. But I am only half a man. I can't give you children. I'm not even sure I can care for you from this contraption as a husband ought to care for a wife."

"Silas McKinnon, will you marry me?" demanded Carol.

Silas laughed and dried his eyes with his handkerchief. "Are you proposing to me?"

"I reckon I am. You're the man I want, and if he won't ask me, I'll have to ask him. A forty-year-old woman gets desperate!"

Silas grasped Carol's head in his massive hands. "I love you, Carol, and I'll give you a hundred percent of whatever's left of me— for the rest of my life." Silas's kiss was eager, hungry, yet gentle.

When he released her, he peered into her eyes. The moment erased the years of waiting, of longing, of grieving over what was and might have been. They were young and alive. In the autumn of their existence, they had the hearts of springtime and the passionate fire of summer love. "I guess, Miss Hicks, the answer is 'Yes.'"

They fed on kisses and tears, until Carol drew back, hesitating before asking, "What will Josiah say? Is this too soon after his mother's death?"

Silas grinned. "Go out on the porch and ring the bell."

"Ring the bell?"

"Go on, woman—do as I say!"

She laughed and moved toward the porch, with Silas's voice trailing after her. "I'm going to have to teach you how to mind a husband—you've been an independent woman too long!"

Carol rang the bell, then returned, asking, "All right, now what was that about?"

"Patience, patience. Come over here and let's practice our kissing some more."

"Silas!" Carol knelt, kissed him, encircled his broad chest with her arms, and laid her head on his chest. "I love you, Silas McKinnon!"

Silas rested his head on hers and stroked her hair. "And I love you, Carol."

The door swung open. "Well, I reckon that means she said 'Yes'!" declared Josiah, followed by the family parade—Sara, Nancy, and Margaret.

"Silas, you mean they knew?"

"Well, I had to ask their permission!" The room was awash in laughter at Carol's expense.

The last trace of doubt flowed out with the relief that washed through Carol. She knew she had been a good sister, a good aunt, a good friend. She had stepped aside for the sake of Peggy's happiness, for the sake of what was right. She had returned in hope of filling the void caused by the deficiencies of Peggy's fractured soul. She had loved and wept and worked and waited, with no anticipation of a moment of reward and happiness such as this.

Carol waved them all to silence. "Now, wait just a minute— Silas McKinnon, did you ask me to marry you?"

Silas looked sheepish. "Not exactly."

"Did I ask you to marry me?" Carol stood with folded arms and waited.

Silas grinned at the group of onlookers. "I believe that's the way it went. All right, all right," confessed Silas. "She asked me, and I said 'Yes.'"

Josiah whistled, and everyone clapped, as Carol gave Silas another kiss.

Margaret called a halt to the pandemonium of hugs and well wishes by declaring, "Enough of this—let's bring in the rest of the food and start the party."

September 1850

Through lips pressed against her needle, Nancy called to her daughter in the opposite bedroom. "Margaret, get Carol's bodice—it's on the back of the chair!"

"Oh, Nancy, my hair!" complained Sara, standing before the bureau, where the oval mirror reflected a face tense with anxiety.

"Your hair is beautiful!" Margaret observed, as she marched into the room carrying the pale blue silk bodice as if it were a gift for the altar.

Taking the garment from Maggie's hands, Nancy commented, "Margaret, you look as lovely as the brides—and about as grown up, I hate to say."

Margaret beamed and replied, "Thank you, Mama. My dress is so pretty." Maggie straightened the lace across her chest and fluffed the puffed undersleeves.

Nancy had made the bodice, jacket, and tiered skirt of the finest pink cotton, edged with white lace; the hem touched the tops of Margaret's slippers—her first long skirt. White lace graced the hem of each tier and the band of the matching pink broad-brimmed hat.

As Nancy helped Carol slide her arms into the bodice, she was reminded of the day the soldiers came, the feel of the exquisite material in her hands, the sheen of silk reflecting the canopy of sky. She had made Carol's dress as a gift for the nearest to a sister she had ever known. The full sweep of white silk skirt was encircled by three wide bands of pale blue silk and lace. Over the matching, pleated, lace-encrusted chemisette, with its bell sleeves puffed to the wrists, the rolled collar of the blue bodice buttoned and was belted at the waist.

"I declare!" exclaimed Nancy, hands resting on her hips. "The folks' eyes will be awhirl trying to look at all three of you beautiful women!"

Carol took Nancy's hand. "Thank you for making this day even more special." Their eyes began to mist, as Carol continued: "I never thought I would ever be—"

"Stop, right there!" ordered Nancy. "You're going to make me cry, and I don't have time for that right now!"

They both laughed and hugged each other.

Nancy directed, "Now, Miss Schoolteacher, set that bonnet on straight, and mind you don't get yourself messed up! Sara, how's the hair coming along?"

Sara sighed. "I think I've got it. How does it look?"

When she turned to assess her daughter, Nancy pressed her mouth with the back of her hand and her face dissolved into sobs.

The creature before her was exquisite in a white silk blouse and matching skirt, gored with lace inserts, studded at the points with pale pink satin rosettes. A tumble of lace ruffles cascaded above the frog closures of the narrow bodice, made of the same pink and embroidered to the waist with vining roses.

"Nancy!" Sara rushed to enfold Nancy in her arms. She teased, "Do I look that bad?"

Nancy shook her head and sniffed, "No, you're beautiful. It's just—we've come so far, and—now you're all grown up."

Sara steeled herself to speak the words she had practiced in her mind for weeks. "Nancy, because of you I am here today. I was lost and scared, until you found me and made me your own. I can never repay you for the love and care you have given me." Sara's voice broke as she concluded. "Thank you, Nancy. I love you."

A few seconds of sniffling passed before Margaret declared, "Look at all of us—I thought today was supposed to be happy, and we're going to be soaked with tears!"

Carol breathed and released a heavy sigh, chuckling, "Our cups are just running over, Maggie!"

Nancy wiped her face. "Well! I believe all of you are ready. I'd best see to myself and double-check the refreshments. We'll leave in twenty minutes."

Carol and Sara followed Nancy and Margaret to the schoolhouse, now rebuilt, refurbished—standing strong and whole with its spire reaching toward heaven.

"Indian summer"—Carol wondered where the term had originated, but she smiled to think how appropriate it was for this blessed day. The late afternoon was mild and warm; cotton puffs of clouds pinned back the drape of azure sky. *How far they had all come!* she thought. Tucked away in this pocket of humanity, they had not only survived, they had flourished. Surely, there had been trials—but, *Blessings*, she thought, *are sometimes only recognized in retrospect.*

As they neared the school building, she saw the preacher on the porch; he was smiling at the approaching assemblage of females as if they were a procession of royal princesses. On the ground near him stood Josiah—handsome, but squirming, in his stiff, high-collared dress shirt. Beside Josiah, in the wheelchair, sat Silas, pensive, yet focused on Carol.

Arriving at the steps, Nancy and Margaret took their places. Josiah turned Silas toward the preacher, then met Sara to give her a bouquet and to take her arm. Carol moved to stand between Josiah and Silas. Looking down at the man she had loved for so long, she smiled and accepted the flowers he gave her.

April 1854

Margaret plopped on the edge of the bed. "But, Mama, I don't want to go to Chattanooga! I want to stay here with Uncle Silas —and with Sara and the baby."

"I know, Margaret, you have made that clear." Nancy stacked her undergarments on the bed along with her toiletries. "But I have discussed it with your Uncle Silas and Aunt Carol. As much as they would miss you, they, too, think it would be good for you to get more education, meet new people—maybe even have the opportunity to go someday to some of those places you like to read about."

"But, Mama," she protested, "I don't want you to leave—not even for a little while."

Nancy combed her fingers through Maggie's hair to reposition the stray tendrils that had come loose from her combs. "Margaret, I have to—just until I see how it is. Sara and Josiah will stay here while I'm away, and you'll have even more time with Samuel. "If there's no place for us there, if I can't get the work I need to support us, then, I'll be back, and we'll go on here as we always have."

Margaret was disconsolate.

Nancy sat next to her and held her hand. "Margaret, you're a bright girl, and there is a world out there we know only through books and newspapers." Maggie leaned against her mother's shoulder. "I'm scared, too, Maggie. I haven't seen Chattanooga since before you were born, and then it was through the pickets of the stockade. I don't know whether there is opportunity there or misery—but I aim to find out before I bring you with me."

Margaret watched as her mother completed her packing and fastened the valise. She thought she had never seen Nancy so beautiful. The wide, flounced crinoline underskirt rustled as she moved and crunched when she leaned against the bed. The bodice of Nancy's dress and the treble skirt were a deep, pure blue, scalloped with black embroidery. Black buttons marched up the front of her bodice to her neck, where the wide lace of her blouse flowed over her shoulders. The wide cuffs of the bell-shaped sleeves, trimmed with the same black embroidery, turned back to expose the lace of the blouse which puffed at her wrists. Nancy's black hair was parted in the middle and smoothed back into the white lace-edged day cap sitting back on her head. Margaret thought that, while there was no way her mother could hide her Cherokee heritage, there was also no way for her to hide her beauty.

"Three months? You promise?" asked Margaret.

"Not one day more—I promise, and I'll write you at least once a week to tell you how things are going. In the meantime, you help Uncle Silas and Aunt Carol and Sara all you can. Be careful of Samuel. I know he's walking now, but that makes him even more a threat to himself."

"I will, Mama."

"I have something for you, Maggie." Nancy pulled open the drawer in the bedside table, retrieved the beaded deerskin purse, and laid it in Maggie's hands.

"Mama, your purse!"

"No, Margaret, now it is your purse. Your father gave it to me when we married, and I have kept it with me all these years. I like to think it carries memories. Now, it is yours. Someday you may pass it to your son or daughter with even more memories—good ones, bad ones. Life is made up of both, but going on, collecting them—that's what we must do."

Margaret rubbed the soft leather between her fingers. "Thank you, Mama." She looked at Nancy, hugged her, and blurted through tears, "I love you."

Nancy choked, "I love you, too." Straightening her back, Nancy stated, "Well, we'd better get my things downstairs. The Daniels will be here soon."

Margaret carried her mother's valise to the porch, while Nancy collected her sewing basket and the crate she had loaded with fabrics and notions.

Nancy and Margaret were just coming out on the porch, as Carol and Sara with the baby came in sight of the house. They all turned at the sound of the carriage approaching from the direction of the school.

"Nancy, wait!" called Carol, and she and Sara ran toward them.

Nancy descended the steps and ran into Carol's outstretched arms. "I'll miss you, Nancy. I'll pray you'll be safe and successful, and I'll write you."

"I'll miss you, too," Nancy responded.

Sara shifted the baby to one arm and moved to hug Nancy. She choked on her words, as she promised her mother, "We'll take good care of Maggie and the house. Don't worry about anything here."

Nancy held their hands. "I love you both. I wouldn't have the courage to do this, if not for you."

"I don't believe that for one moment, my friend," laughed Carol. "Chattanooga may find itself retaken by one lone Cherokee woman!"

"Nancy, you ready?" called Mr. Daniel, the new head of the mine, recently bought by a Cincinnati company. He had loaded Nancy's bags and carton and stood ready to assist her into the carriage.

"Be right there, Mr. Daniel!" Nancy gave the baby a kiss on the cheek and said, "I love you, sweet Samuel." Nancy turned to give Maggie one last hug and kiss. "I love you, child. Three months, maybe less, I promise. I don't think I could bear being away from you any longer." Nancy caressed Maggie's face and kissed her again on the forehead. "Goodbye."

"Goodbye, Mama," Maggie whispered.

Mr. Daniel helped Nancy maneuver her skirts into the carriage, where she took her place next to his wife, who was garbed in the rose bodice and skirt with ivory lace trim Nancy had finished only the previous week.

Mr. Daniel slapped the reins, and the carriage rolled eastward to Chattanooga. Nancy had left Ross's Landing a homeless Cherokee squaw, as the soldier had called her, in sweat-soaked, bloodstained gray homespun. She was returning a landed, middle-class widow woman, in finery befitting the streets of Charleston. All that remained unchanged were the high bronze cheekbones, the penetrating black eyes, and the carriage of the proud, strong back.

Mr. Daniel reigned the horses to a halt before the address Nancy had given him. The milliner's shop was on a side street, just around the corner from the Hotel Chattanooga.

"Mr. Daniel, do you mind waiting just a moment?" she asked.

"I'll be right here. Take your time. Mrs. Daniel will be a while at the cabinet makers."

A bell jingled as Nancy opened the door to the shop, which was arranged as a comfortable, inviting parlor. She admired the latest colorful creations displayed on hat stands set about on marble-topped tables and on an ornate, carved sideboard to her left. In a few moments, a tall, stylish black woman of regal bearing appeared from behind a dressing screen at the rear of the shop.

"May I help you?" she asked, as she scanned Nancy from bonnet to hem.

"Mrs. Lancaster?"

"Miss Lancaster," she corrected Nancy.

"Miss Lancaster, I am Nancy Hilderbrand. I responded to your advertisement in the *Gazette*—for a dressmaker." Taking a folded letter from the pocket in her jacket, Nancy opened it and showed it to the woman. "You responded that you would like to meet and consider me for the position."

"Yes, I did. I didn't realize you were—"

"Indian?" Nancy interrupted.

"Well—yes," she admitted.

Nancy retorted, "Cherokee—and I didn't expect you to be black, but I see you are, nevertheless, quite an exceptional milliner."

"Touché—and thank you." The woman walked around Nancy, perusing her dress. "Did you make these clothes?"

"Yes, ma'am, I did—I'm good at what I do, and I try to stay abreast of the latest fashions."

Miss Lancaster picked up the hem of Nancy's skirt to assess the hem stitching. She nodded, pursed her lips, and asked, "Are you fast?"

"As fast as I can be and still do quality work."

Miss Lancaster smiled. "Me too. My customers know my time and their money can produce a mighty fine hat. Come. Sit down. I'll get us a cup of tea, and we'll talk."

"Thank you, I'd like that." Miss Lancaster was on her way behind the screen, when Nancy stopped her. "Excuse me—do you happen to know where I might find a room for the night? The friend who brought me is waiting, and I need to tell him where to deliver my bags."

"Tell him to bring them in. I have two apartments upstairs. I live in one, and the other is unoccupied right now. We'll work the rent into our agreement."

Nancy was trying to sort her thoughts, as she stuffed tissue into the bosom and arms of the Canezou. Tiers of lace covered the breast of the dainty cambric shirt and fell from the cuffs of the bell–shaped sleeves. The stiffened, lace trimmed collar would frame Mrs. Anderson's long, graceful neck; and its lines, coming to a point at the belted waist, would accentuate her reed-slim figure.

"Here we go," said Opal Lancaster as she handed the matching day cap to Nancy. "That looks lovely," she remarked as she assessed the garment Nancy was arranging for delivery. Let's pack the hat separately. I want Mrs. Anderson to see that neckline when she opens the box."

Nancy turned to retrieve a small hatbox from the shelf of supplies.

"You're mighty quiet today, Nancy," Opal commented.

Nancy smiled. "I guess I just have a lot on my mind."

"Margaret?"

Nancy nodded. "I enjoy my work. You have been gracious and generous. But I promised Margaret this would be the month I would come home—either to stay or to gather her up to bring her back."

"Which will it be?"

Nancy shook her head. "I want to come back, but I haven't found a place for Margaret—for her education, for friends. What is there here for her? I am content to work on my designs, to see the satisfaction of our customers." She chuckled. "I even am amused at the way heads swivel at the hotel, when this well-turned-out Indian woman parades through the lobby with her packages. Collecting the money they're willing to pay is better than collecting scalps!"

As their laughter died, Nancy added, "But what would Margaret have?"

"I'll understand, Nancy, if you decide to go home. But I couldn't replace you." Opal paused and watched while Nancy put the lids on the boxes and began tying them with twine. "You know, if you decide you must go back to Shake Rag, maybe we could work something out with the Daniels. They come in just about every month for a couple of days. Maybe I could send you orders and the materials you need by them, and they could return your work the next time they're in town."

"You'd be willing to do that?"

"Like I said, I couldn't replace you."

Nancy lowered her head and finished tying a knot. "You don't know how much that offer means to me."

"Think about it," said Opal.

"I will. Thank you." Nancy took her bonnet from the hall tree, removed the white gloves from inside it, and slipped her fingers into them. Popping the cap on her head, she tied the bow with a flourish under her chin and declared, "Time to sally forth into enemy territory."

"Keep your chin up and your eyes down," Opal directed, "like this," she demonstrated.

Laughing, Nancy picked up the stack of boxes, squared her shoulders, and mimicked Opal. "Quite right, Miss Lancaster. See you later in the afternoon."

By now, Nancy was used to the greetings of familiar faces and the stares of strangers as she circled the corner and made her way to the entrance of the hotel, where carriages were discharging fine ladies, many brandishing parasols, and their collections of baggage. Most of their men were hustling about their business on foot, and Nancy wondered if it were out of courtesy they relinquished the transportation, or if they were merely escaping the billowing skirts, the sunshades, the luggage, and the vacuous chatter and preening.

Nancy proceeded into the lobby with a nod and a smile to the doorman, who likewise greeted her. Crossing to the desk, she set her boxes on the counter and waited for the attention of the clerk, who was attending a tall figure in a gray coat, wheat-colored trousers and vest, and holding a gray hat. Nancy caught a glimpse of a blue cravat encircling white silk at the neck.

While the man registered, the clerk turned to her. "Yes, Nancy?"

"Mr. McNeal, I have a delivery for Mrs. Anderson."

The man at the register glanced at Nancy and then, surprised, looked again, as Mr. McNeal replied, "Go on up, Nancy, she's expecting you."

The man in gray finished his signature with a flourish and accepted the key from Mr. McNeal. Nancy gathered up her boxes and made her way to the stairs.

"Ma'am, excuse me, ma'am!"

Nancy stopped and turned to see the man in gray coming toward her.

He pushed back the brown hair from his forehead and apologized. "Excuse me for being so bold, but I heard you say you were going to Mrs. Anderson's suite. I am James Dunwoody, Mrs. Anderson's brother. I am in the adjoining room, and I thought I might deliver the boxes for you—Miss?"

"*Mrs.* Hilderbrand. Thank you, Mr. Dunwoody, but I must collect payment for these." Nancy continued on her way.

"Mrs. Hilderbrand!" The man approached her again. "Please, at least let me carry the packages for you. I would be such a lout to let a petite lady like you carry these packages up three floors when I am going the same way."

"Well, all right, Mr. Dunwoody. I would not want you to appear loutish, though I am well able to manage."

"I am sure you are but thank you." He placed his hat on his head and took the boxes from her.

They made their way up the first flight of stairs.

"Are you from around here, Mrs. Hilderbrand?"

"Yes."

"How is it—how did you—"

"Did you think we were all run out, Mr. Dunwoody?"

"Let's say, I feared so."

Nancy stopped and looked at the man with the clear blue eyes and kind smile.

He explained, "I was not a friend of Jackson. He ran roughshod over our entire system of justice."

"Thank you. It's satisfying to hear that coming from a gentleman like yourself." Nancy continued up the next flight.

"Perhaps, sometime, you would be kind enough to tell me about your people—and your view of the Removal."

"Mr. Dunwoody, my people are only my immediate family, and the Removal was long ago."

"I'm sorry, I was being very presumptuous. Please, forgive me."

Nancy looked at the man whose face was blushing with innocent embarrassment. She stopped on the landing and waited for him to face her. "Mr. Dunwoody, my husband was killed in the Removal. For many years, I have tried to rid myself of anger and hatred. I have come a long way since that time."

"I'm sorry, Mrs. Hilderbrand—truly."

There was something about his blue eyes that reminded her of Silas—perhaps, it was the earnest, honest emotion they could not conceal. Like Silas, he seemed to be an open heart, susceptible to injury, yet ready to bleed for others. She relented. "Mr. Dunwoody, sometime, I would be willing to answer any questions you might have."

"Would you have tea with me in the dining room this afternoon?"

Nancy ascended the last group of stairs. "Mr. Dunwoody," she smiled, "you are, certainly, very curious!"

He laughed. "I'm only going to be here a few days. I have no time to waste!"

Nancy stopped at the third floor. "Mr. Dunwoody, I would have tea with you, but you must stop to consider the effect that might have on any of your associates who might see you. A gentleman like you, having tea with an Indian woman …"

"But you are a beautiful, elegant lady!" he blurted.

Nancy was frozen with astonishment.

"Oh—Mrs. Hilderbrand," he stammered, "I am truly sorry." He avoided her gaze as he hastened along the hall, while saying, "Sometimes, I just speak without thinking. Please, excuse me."

Nancy followed Mr. Dunwoody to Mrs. Anderson's suite. The door was opened after his knock, just as she arrived to meet him.

"James! We've been expecting you!" Mrs. Anderson's mellifluous voice betrayed her Charleston breeding. She gave her brother a kiss on the cheek and asked, "And what is all this?"

James returned his sister's kiss and replied, "Well, frankly, sister, I have no idea. I just offered to assist this lady with her delivery." He stepped aside so Charlotte Anderson might see the figure of her seamstress standing behind him.

"Nancy, come in!" Mrs. Anderson motioned for her to enter the well-appointed suite. "James, this is Nancy Hilderbrand, just about the finest dress stylist this side of Charleston. I will never understand how this town came to be blessed with a woman of her talent!"

"Thank you, Mrs. Anderson. I hope you are pleased."

Relieving her brother of the packages, Charlotte said, "James, let me set these over here on the settee. I must show you her handiwork."

Nancy observed the affection of the brother and sister as he knelt on one knee and placed his arm around Charlotte on the back of her seat. Charlotte's delicate white fingers set the smaller box aside, untied the twine of the larger, and removed the lid. Turning back the tissue covering the lace confection, she gasped, "Oh, it's the loveliest thing!" She pulled the blouse up by the shoulders to give James a clearer view. "See, didn't I tell you? She's wonderful!"

James Dunwoody caught Nancy's eye and grinned. "I must agree."

For the first time, Nancy wondered if blushing was apparent on her Cherokee face. "Mrs. Anderson, I must be getting back to the shop. If you would check the day cap to see if it is to your satisfaction. Also, the bill is in the hat box."

"Of course, Nancy—"

A door burst open from what appeared to be a bedroom and scurrying into the parlor came two girls—one blonde, one red-haired—followed by a young boy Nancy recognized as Charlotte's son, Albert, who was the very image of his mother.

"Daddy! You're here!" The red-haired girl dashed to James Dunwoody, as he rose to his feet to meet her with an embrace that lifted her off the floor.

"Ginny! Oh, but it's good to see you!"

Nancy was perplexed.

"Nancy, this is my niece, Virginia." She gestured toward the young lady in her father's arms. "And this is my daughter, Lydia. They just arrived here from Charleston. They have been staying with my parents until our house here was finished. James just returned from business up in Pennsylvania. Virginia will be staying with us a few months while James is traveling. He is involved with my husband in getting the iron works up and going. Girls, this is Mrs. Hilderbrand, our dressmaker."

"She's a real Indian!" blurted Albert.

"Albert!" Charlotte scolded.

James released Virginia and she turned to join Lydia in staring at Nancy.

Nancy was amused by their shocked expressions.

"Nancy, please excuse the children," Charlotte apologized. "They have been so interested in the history of this part of the country, and then to meet a Cherokee—well, they have forgotten their manners."

Lydia came forward. "Mrs. Hilderbrand, please excuse me. You are just not at all what I expected—I mean—oh, I'm sorry, I don't know what I mean." Flustered, she held her reddened face in her hands.

Nancy chuckled. "It's quite all right, Lydia. I have a daughter just about your age, I would guess. She, also, doesn't know what she is saying sometimes."

Virginia interrupted, "May we meet her, Mrs. Hilderbrand? I would love to tell my friends back in Charleston I have a real Indian for a friend."

Nancy glanced at Charlotte Anderson, who rolled her eyes, then looked at Nancy in embarrassment.

"My daughter is not with me, Virginia. In fact, I will be leaving very soon to return to my home along the Narrows."

"What?" exclaimed Mrs. Anderson. "You're leaving? But why? I hope people have not been unkind to you. Has your business gone well?"

"No, on the whole, I have been well-treated. And business has been very good for Miss Lancaster and myself. It's just that I had hoped to find a place for Margaret, my daughter, for her education, and I have found none. And she is happy where she is. I promised I would be away only three months, and that time is about up."

"Oh, Nancy, I am so sorry you're leaving! Of course, I must admit, that's largely for selfish reasons. Just look at this lovely creation, girls!" Charlotte Anderson held up the garment.

Nancy noticed James Dunwoody standing with his chin in his hand as he studied the scene of females fluttering over the package of lace and frills. His eyes seemed to brighten, and then he announced, "Charlotte, I have asked Mrs. Hilderbrand if she will have tea and tell us about herself. I am sure we would find that tremendously interesting. Do you think we could invite her for tea tomorrow afternoon? We could have it served up here, where we might relax and not be rushed."

"Oh, mother, that is a wonderful idea!" exclaimed Lydia.

"Could we Aunt Charlotte?" Virginia pleaded.

"I think that would be lovely, if Nancy can arrange to come," agreed Charlotte Anderson.

Nancy's response was polite, but cool. "Thank you, but I'm afraid I have quite a bit of work to finish tomorrow." Nancy made her way to the door. "I can let myself out. It was a pleasure to meet you—Lydia, Virginia—Mr. Dunwoody." Nancy closed the door behind her and hastened down the hall.

Nancy had thought she was immune to the pain of prejudice. These people had seemed so friendly, so accepting—but Mr. Dunwoody's suggestion that she be invited to tea and then be hidden away in their apartment touched a raw nerve. "Mrs. Hilderbrand! Wait! Please!" James Dunwoody's voice called to her as she was descending the stairs.

She stopped. He caught his breath before speaking. "It seems I am always beseeching you to stop!"

"Yes, Mr. Dunwoody?"

"You forgot your payment." He handed her some folded bills.

"Thank you." Nancy turned away.

"Mrs. Hilderbrand, please! Did I say something to offend you?"

Nancy faced him. "Mr. Hilderbrand, your invitation to tea was generous, but I am not an oddity to be hidden from the public for your private amusement."

"Oh, you mean the change in my invitation!" He huffed and shook his head. "Why don't I think! Mrs. Hilderbrand—please, let me explain. A moment ago, I had an idea concerning your daughter's education—I think you might find it intriguing. I wanted to discuss it with my family before presenting it to you. I thought we could all talk more freely in the suite tomorrow."

Nancy considered his words.

"Mrs. Hilderbrand, I assure you, I have no qualms about being seen with you anywhere. In fact, if you will allow me, after our tea and visit tomorrow, I would like to invite you to have dinner with me downstairs."

Nancy was confused. "Mr. Dunwoody, I don't think I should—aren't you a married man—your daughter?"

"Mrs. Hilderbrand, my wife, Lily, died of consumption when Ginny was only three."

* * * * * * * * *

Nancy's hands trembled as she closed the last black frog on the rose bodice. Her desire to overlook no opportunity for Margaret—and curiosity—were motivating her to go, though her courage had frayed threads of fear. She shook the black taffeta skirt and smoothed it over the crinoline. She adjusted the black-embroidered white collar around her face and tied the bow of the pert day cap at just the right angle under her chin. Leaning into the mirror to get a better view, she screwed the backs of the silver dangles at her ears. She thought, *Well, if dressing the part means anything, I'm ready!*

"Excuse me, did you see my associate, Mrs. Hilderbrand, up there?" Opal inquired, as Nancy descended the stair from their apartments.

"Oh, that little old dressmaker? I left her up there somewhere," she quipped.

"Mind if I put a placard on you for advertisement while you are sashaying around the hotel?"

"Want me to give out cigars and candy too?"

Opal's teasing and smooth contralto laughter eased Nancy's nerves. "Here, you might want to take this." Opal handed her a black and white parasol.

"Opal! No, I don't think so!"

"Now, it's just what you need to complete your attire, Lady Hilderbrand."

"Thank you, but I draw the fashion line at parasols!"

Opal shrugged. "Have it your way."

Nancy opened the shop door.

"Nancy!" Opal called.

Nancy turned.

"You look beautiful, Nancy. You can hold your own with anyone, anywhere."

Nancy smiled. "Thanks."

"So, you see, Nancy," James Dunwoody explained, "twice a week you could bring Margaret to be tutored with our daughters. Mr. Atchley is a very well-educated professor of all subjects, including music, Latin, deportment. A couple of years with him would give Margaret an excellent finishing."

"And the cost? I am not a woman of wealth, Mr. Dunwoody."

James Dunwoody nodded to his sister across the tea table.

"Nancy, we want you, too, to teach our children. I realize you must think the girls and me a lot of silly, shallow females—we appear to be, I know. But..." Charlotte searched for words.

"Mrs. Hilderbrand, my sister and I are of like minds, in that we are concerned that our children grow in character and spirit—learn values and skills that will serve them well as human beings. I'm a Citadel graduate myself—one of the best educations available to a man. Albert will have that opportunity. But we want our daughters to have an education beyond dead languages, sonnets, and deportment and etiquette. We don't want them prepared only to hobnob with people who can't see beyond their porcelain tea cups."

"What can I teach them? All I know is sewing."

"That, in part," responded Charlotte. "Why can't the girls learn to sew and embroider? What a sense of satisfaction it must give you to make something fine enough to wear!"

"And the history of your people, Nancy," added James. "I know there may still be a great deal of pain associated with the past, but don't lose the riches of your heritage. There is so much we all would like to know, to learn. Perhaps, you might even allow us to visit your home along the river."

"I don't know, Mr. Dunwoody. It seems you are getting very little in return for your investment in my daughter's education."

"One more enticement to help you make your decision— when I return, I am bringing one of the new sewing machines. It will be placed in the workroom off Charlotte's kitchen. Once you learn the operation of it, we would like for you to teach the girls—one afternoon a week, the use of the machine—also, other sewing skills and the culture and history of your people. On the two days you come for Margaret's lessons, you may have free access to the machine to do any work you have. It likely would help your production tremendously."

Nancy studied her teacup, then asked, "What about the children? How do they feel about all this? And, if I may be frank, how will they feel about associating with Cherokees on such an intimate basis? My daughter is an intelligent, sensitive girl. I could not bear her being shamed or ridiculed."

Charlotte admonished, "Nancy, children are going to be children. I cannot guarantee they will never say anything that might offend. And they are curious—they will ask questions. But, we trust, they are neither mean nor hateful—nor do they judge a man by the color of his skin."

James Dunwoody added, "This is, perhaps, a bit off subject, but you might be interested to know our family in Charleston does not own slaves. They employ some free blacks in their household staff, but they receive fair compensation for their work. Now, don't get me wrong—I'm a States' Rights man, but I part company with my fellow-thinkers on the matter of slavery. Besides, my growing business with the iron industry in Pennsylvania has made it my adopted home. I must say, the convictions of the anti-slavery movement there have only solidified my thinking on the matter."

Nancy sipped her tea and thought, *Challenge, temptation, opportunity—sometimes only in hindsight is one distinguishable from the other.*

"Mrs. Anderson, Mr. Dunwoody—I promised Margaret three months, then I would either come home to stay or come home to get her and bring her back. I will see if she will give me the same—a three-month trial period, to come to Chattanooga to see if this is what she wants."

Charlotte Anderson breathed a sigh of relief. "Nancy, thank you. I think that is a very fair offer." She extended her hand to Nancy.

"Yes, thank you, Nancy," added James. "May I call you 'Nancy'? 'Mrs. Hilderbrand' seems to get longer on my tongue every time I speak it!"

Nancy laughed and said, "Of course," as she extended her hand to James Dunwoody.

"Well, James," announced Charlotte, "I think we can call the children to join us. Prepare yourself, Nancy—they are going to be very excited."

* * * * * * * * *

"I am Mr. Dunwoody. I have a table reserved for two."

Nancy looked around the quiet, darkened dining room, where, on each table, candles glowed in globes embedded in fresh flowers. The muted chatter of voices faded as faces turned in their direction.

"Ah—Mr. Dunwoody—let me see—are you quite sure you placed your reservation?" In his confusion, the man, looking nervous and uncomfortable in his starched white collar, searched for the name on his list.

"Yes, but if you need confirmation, I am sure the manager will be happy to provide it. My sister, Mrs. Anderson, and I are staying in adjoining suites on the third floor."

"Oh, yes, the Andersons. Well, I'm sure it's here. If you will follow me, please." Glancing this way and that at patrons in passing, the headwaiter escorted them toward the back of the dining room.

"The table in the garden nook," directed James Dunwoody, "over there, if it isn't taken."

"Why, no—no, sir. This way, please."

The headwaiter led them to the table, which gave them privacy, yet a view of the restaurant. He pulled the chair from the table for Nancy, then allowed James to be seated before offering him a menu.

James waved it away and said, "We'll have the table d'hote for two and water with lemon. We'll have coffee with our dessert later."

When the headwaiter moved away, Nancy asked, "Do you know what you ordered?"

James grinned. "No, but it's usually the best they have to offer. Besides, it's just food—an excuse to be with you."

"Mr. Dunwoody! Again, you are not thinking before you speak."

"James."

"All right, James."

"I told you, my time here is short." He laughed.

Nancy smiled and fiddled with her napkin.

"I've embarrassed you. I'm sorry."

"It's just that…you leave me at a loss for words, and…I've never had dinner with a man like this—in public, before."

"Well, I want to make you so comfortable doing this, you will have dinner with me whenever I am in town."

"I don't know—"

"By the way," he interrupted, "please note our table— privacy for our conversation, yet"— he gestured around the room— "you may see them—but, better for them, they may see you—the most beautiful woman in the room."

"Mr. Dunwoody!"

"James," he corrected.

"James."

"Nancy, I am so pleased you have accepted our offer—at least, on a trial basis. I hope you and Margaret will find it a most agreeable arrangement."

"We will see—I can promise nothing. But, as much as Margaret loves our home and family, she has dreams and intelligence to make her dreams come true—given an education and opportunity. We will see."

"I am just happy I have three months in which to see you from time to time."

"Mr.—James, are you always this forward? We met only yesterday."

"I'm sorry, I have been forward—but you are a fascinating woman."

"Would I be so fascinating without this Cherokee face?" Nancy felt a twinge of irritation.

"A bit less, perhaps," he retorted with a grin.

His honesty melted Nancy's reservation and made her laugh. "You remind me of my daughter. Her mind, also, has trouble keeping up with her tongue."

"I look forward to meeting a fellow free-speaker." He raised his glass in a mock toast. "Seriously, Nancy, please don't think badly of me. Things have seemed to come together for me lately—the ironworks, Charlotte's move here, where I can see more of Ginny." He followed the embroidered design of the tablecloth. "Since Lily died, I have not been a very good father. Thanks to my parents and Charlotte, Ginny has not wanted for anything—except me. Now, I hope to change that."

"It is very difficult to lose the mates of our youth."

"Yes—it is. When Lily died, I determined to bury myself in work. But Ginny is a young lady now. She is going to be grown and gone before long—I must seize every moment with her I can. So, the point I was about to make is that things have seemed to be going so well, I naturally assumed meeting you was just another shower of good fortune."

"Fate?"

"Well, something like that."

"And fate has not brought you someone more…" Nancy searched for words. "Like yourself?"

James chuckled. "No, Charlotte has tried to arrange meetings with friends and relatives of her social circle—but, no. I think I felt, if I couldn't have Lily, I would just have work that satisfied me." He leaned closer to whisper, "Let me tell you a secret—you are the first woman with whom I have dined alone since Lily died—well, except for Ginny or Charlotte, of course. So, in a way, this is a first for both of us."

Nancy was beginning to feel uncomfortable again. "James—let me be very honest. I do not want to encourage any romantic pursuit on your part. I am not sure I want to be involved with another man. The pain of losing David was almost more than I could bear. I don't want to feel that much pain again."

"I understand, Nancy—"

The waiter delivered bowls of steak soup, encrusted with cheese, and sprinkled with browned onions.

James took a deep breath to inhale the vapor of the steaming broth. "Ah— remember what I said about the food's being just an excuse to be with you?"

Nancy nodded.

"Well, I'm afraid this soup is cause for me to retract that statement."

Nancy, again at ease, teased, "This soup is cause for me to want to spend a great deal of time with my new, very good friend, James."

James extended his hand. "I'll settle for that—friend Nancy."

October 1860

"Mother, are you going to join the throng flocking to hear Mr. Short britches, or are you going to listen to the hoopla from here?" Having canceled her tutoring appointments because of the arrival of Stephen Douglas, Margaret had offered the day to assist Opal and Nancy at L & H Clothiers, now ensconced in an elegant, sedate storefront off the lobby of the Hotel Chattanooga. The plush carpet, ornate Victorian settee, and floral armchairs invited leisurely comfort and relaxed viewing of the latest designs in chapeaux and fashion but belied the industrious bustle and whirl of women and machines in the rear of the shop, concealed from view by velvet swag curtains and a Chinoiserie screen.

"With the brass bands blaring and the troops marching through the streets, I think I'll get a feel for things from here. I may venture a peek out the lobby." Nancy's deft fingers guided the woolen fabric under the needle of the machine as she spoke.

"Well, I'd be right there in the middle of things, if it weren't for Mrs. Stevens wanting to pick up this hat for the reception this evening," injected Opal.

Nancy advised, "James says we're heading for war—it's inevitable. You may not want to be in the middle of things then." She clipped the threads with her shears and turned the facing of the dress collar.

"Well, Mr. Dunwoody better be flipping his coin to determine which side of this thing he's going to be on." Opal retorted. "From what you say, he's a divided man."

"James is a good man who hates slavery, but he also doesn't want the Federal government sticking its nose into business. He'd like to see a peaceful resolution to all this, but things in South Carolina are heating up again." Nancy held up the top to the emerald green and black-striped wool for inspection. "He says he'd like to have Ginny back here in Chattanooga—thinks it will be a safer place to be. But she's set on staying in Charleston to be near that fellow she met last summer."

Margaret added, "Lily says he's a cotton broker and is, surely, going to be right in there with the secessionists, if it comes to that."

Nancy shook her head. "I know, and James is anxious about that, too. He's afraid Ginny's going to up and marry the man, with no thought of what the future holds."

"And we wouldn't want to be up and marrying a man now, would we, Mother?" Margaret taunted.

"And what do you mean by that, pray tell?" Nancy's machine stopped, and she cocked her hands on her hips.

"Just that poor Mr. Dunwoody has waited for you to come around for years. And it's apparent to everyone but you, that you care for him a great deal, too—am I right, Opal?"

"Now, Margaret, don't be drawing me into the matchmaking business. I have my hands full, thank you." Then Opal looked at

Nancy and grinned. "But his name surely does come up a might in conversation!"

"Well, he's smitten, if you ask me!" Margaret declared, turning again to her work.

"Smitten or not, we are just very good friends. I made that clear—way back—good friends and nothing more." Brandishing shears from the tips of her fingers, Nancy tried to wave away the subject.

"Uncle Silas says that's the basis of a beautiful marriage."

"Margaret—enough!" Nancy ordered.

Margaret shrugged her shoulders and winked at Opal, who said nothing and refocused on the chapeau. Margaret continued with her arrangement of bolts of material according to fabric and spools of thread according to color. She wondered how her mother and Opal found anything in the workroom, as chaotic as it became at times. But, then, creative people were not supposed to be well organized, especially with impatient ladies waiting for custom designs. Besides, in recent months, her mother seemed to have barely enough energy for sewing, much less for the physical labor of maintenance around the shop. Nancy practically crawled up the stairs in the evenings and often went straight to bed without a bite of supper.

The doorbell chimed. "I'll see to it," offered Margaret.

"Thanks. I don't know how we'd manage without you today," Opal sighed.

Margaret teased, as she hastened to the front, "I don't know how you two alone manage it any day!" She stepped through the curtain and around a screen to confront a large box on the legs of a deliveryman, obscured, except for his hands and intense blue eyes peeping around the side under a mop of unruly black hair.

"Delivery for you, ma'am."

Margaret was startled—it might have been Uncle Silas's voice, with a more pronounced lilt.

"Just set it down over here." Margaret motioned to an area of floor space nearest the workroom.

"Whew! Mighty glad to have that one grounded!" he laughed.

Margaret signed the delivery ticket. "Excuse me, but are you from Scotland? I noticed your dialect is much like my uncle's."

"Why, yes, ma'am—might say, fresh off the boat. Came here to be with my uncle—Henry McNeal, the desk clerk. He paid my passage."

"It's good to hear you speak. I visited my Uncle Silas just this past summer, but I miss him already." She extended her hand. "My name is Margaret—Margaret Hilderbrand."

The deliveryman rubbed his hand on the hip of his pants and took her hand. "Thomas McNeal—and I knew who you were before you even told me."

"You did?"

"Yes, ma'am, my Uncle Henry told me about the Cherokee lady and her daughter who worked here—and he was right."

"About what?"

"Said one was the spittin' image of the other, and both as pretty as you'll find anywhere this side of the ocean. Haven't seen your mother, but she must be a fair woman, indeed!"

"You even have my uncle's way with words, Thomas McNeal!"

Nancy interrupted their laughter by appearing from the workroom to ask, "Well, Margaret, who do we have here?"

"Mother, this is Thomas McNeal, nephew of Mr. McNeal, the desk clerk. Thomas brought this package for you. Wait till you hear his voice."

"Thomas, I am pleased to meet you." She extended her hand.

"Mrs. Hilderbrand, it is an honor to meet you. My uncle has spoken of you with great respect and admiration."

"Why, thank you—and I see what you mean, Margaret—reminiscent of Uncle Silas."

"I'm happy to be a pleasant reminder of a fellow-countryman." Thomas backed toward the door. "Well, Mrs. Hilderbrand, Miss Hilderbrand, I'd best be moving along. I have a few more errands."

"Are you working here now, Thomas?" Nancy questioned.

"Just helping out temporarily. I'm expecting to go on with the ironworks in a few days."

"Are you a foundry man?" asked Margaret.

"Not for long, I trust. I'm a farmer at heart. I'll work till I make enough for some land, and then I'll be getting my hands back in the soil."

"Well, stop by anytime, Thomas—delivery or not," Nancy directed. "We keep a pot of tea or coffee on hand most all the time."

"Thank you, ma'am." He reached for the doorknob. "Good day, ladies," he nodded as he let himself out.

Margaret followed him to the door and peered through the glass. "Wasn't he just the handsomest man, Mother?"

"Margaret Hilderbrand!" Nancy exclaimed. "Here you are, practically on the verge of being an old maid—finally, a man piques your interest! Thought I'd never see the day!"

Sashaying toward the workroom, Margaret returned her teasing. "I figured you and Aunt Carol and Sara had captured all the good men—but maybe I was wrong."

When they returned to their chores, Opal was still fussing over Mrs. Stevens' bonnet. "What's all this talk about men I'm hearing in here?"

Nancy rolled her eyes and replied, as she seated herself at the machine and arranged the fold of fabric under the needle, "Margaret has taken to the deliveryman, who has the lilting voice and blue eyes of her Uncle Silas."

"Uh-oh, Margaret, men are trouble and toil—better be careful!"

"Is that why you never married, Opal—trouble and toil?" Margaret asked, as she perched over the stand where Opal was arranging a sweep of feathers along the brim of the hat.

"No, Margaret." Opal became serious, thoughtful. "I loved a man once—long time ago." She avoided Margaret's eyes. "He was not free. His master took him down into Georgia somewhere. We never saw each other again."

Margaret placed her hand on Opal's. "I'm sorry."

"Oh, child, don't you be apologizing for anything. Looks to me like we all are in about the same boat. The government snatched you away from your land, just like the slave traders snatched my grandpa away from his. But we take what comes and make the best of it. My daddy worked hard and bought his freedom and my mother's; he bought my older brother; he's still buying up family as he finds them."

Nancy's machine was silent as she listened to Opal speak. In the six years she had worked for Opal—even in the last several months they had been partners, she had never known Opal to reveal so much of her personal life. She spoke up, "Well, I pray, if war is coming, it brings with it freedom for your people."

Opal sighed. "I do, too, but I fear it may come at an awful cost."

"I am confused by all of this—I don't know who is right or wrong!" Margaret voiced her exasperation, "I hate slavery and what it has done to your family, but I hate Jackson for what he did—and

197

his kind, too. Like those who are crying 'Union' and 'Freedom' now, Jackson was a Nationalist, yet he was a slave owner. And those who want States Rights would have upheld what Georgia did in stealing Cherokee land."

"That's the way of man, it seems," Opal mused. "When it's all said and done, most men just want to line their pockets—even if it be with other men's money, at the expense of other men's sweat and misery."

"That's why it's a hard time for good men like James," Nancy interjected. "It's difficult to decide on which side to take a stand."

"That's why," concluded Opal, "freedom to me is the only issue worth considering." The hatpin in her hand waved as she spoke. "Even as a free black, I'm not free. My daddy and I could buy out most any of the whites in this county, but we have to get a white agent to handle our business affairs—our name on the paper's not good enough, even with money in the bank!"

Nancy reflected on her purchase of land from Silas. She had signed nothing, but he had presented her with a deed—proper, recorded, stating she owned her home and surrounding acreage. He presented a similar deed to Caroline for the school and land on the other side of the trail. She wondered if it had been courtesy on Silas's part that he had transacted the business for them, or if he had accomplished the sale to Cherokees in the only way possible.

Freedom? Nancy wondered just how free she was. She remembered the confines of the stockade—the misery of summer heat, the cries and coughs of illness, the wails of the bereaved, the dreaded travail of the journey to the West, the expectation of disease, of death. Determined to free herself and her child from that captivity, she had vowed she would never again be bound. Her wits and her skills would raise her above the shackles of the spirit, and her soul would be free—if she had to sacrifice her body to have it so. But, was there a freedom that was not hers to claim— not hers by right or design or will, but that had to be bestowed on her by some beneficent legality?

"Mother, are you all right?" asked Margaret.

"What?"

"You were in a daze."

"Oh, I was just thinking." Nancy's feet moved again on the treadle.

"Well, I tell you, I've about got Mrs. Stevens' hat finished. I may move myself along down to the depot to hear what Douglas has to say." Opal held up the hat stand and turned it to inspect the cap from all angles." She tied the bow and adjusted the streamers to be of matching length. "Sure, I can't persuade you to come with me, Nancy?"

"No, I think I'll stay here. You go on. I'll try to finish the bodice on this dress."

"Margaret?"

"Thanks, I'll stay with mother for now. I might go out on the sidewalk after a while."

Opal collected her bonnet, shawl, and purse. "I'll be seeing you all later, then."

Nancy called, "Opal! Please, be careful!"

Opal waved and closed the door behind her.

"Mother, what do you really think about all this—secession, a war, I mean?"

"I think we might just go back home."

"Why, I thought you said James wanted Ginny to come here because it would be safer."

"I know—and maybe he's right—maybe safer than Charleston with its port and cotton trade. But the way I see it, with the railroads through here now, the river traffic—armies need supplies and troops—how are they going to move them? Seems to me the straightest shot between the north and the south is right through Chattanooga."

"Have you suggested this to James?"

"Not yet, but I will when I write back to him."

Margaret busied herself with sweeping threads and clippings around Nancy. "Mother, would you never consider marrying again?"

"Why all this interest in my romantic life lately?" Nancy did not look up from her stitching.

"It just seems you might want someone for companionship as you grow old."

"I have my work."

Margaret stopped sweeping and rested her chin on the broom handle. "Mother, what if your eyes fail you? What if your hands become arthritic? What if you can't work anymore?"

"I'll have our home and some savings."

Margaret was becoming frustrated. "Well, you'll be sheltered from the elements, but savings won't give you companionship—or warm your feet under the covers on a cold night!"

"Margaret!"

The broom wobbled in Margaret's hand, as she orated, "Well, it's true! And James is just about the kindest man I've known, since Uncle Silas—and he loves you!"

Nancy seemed transfixed by the outburst from her daughter.

"Oh, I know, you think you can love no one as you loved my father. When I was young, David Hilderbrand was my hero—practically an immortal. Now, I realize he was a good man, who loved his wife and child and died bravely trying to protect them, like any good man would, just like James would."

Nancy shook her head and studied a seam. "You don't understand, Margaret."

"I guess I don't." Margaret swept the pile of scraps into the dustpan.

Nancy sighed. "Margaret, come here."

Margaret propped the broom against the shelf and stood in front of her mother, who took her hands in her own.

"Margaret, you're a grown woman now and should understand. I care for James very much. He is a fine man and a good friend, and I will forever be grateful to him for your education. But I don't want to love again—not as I loved your father. My heart was laid open, completely. All I wanted was to feel his arms around me, and that is how he died. I awoke lying in the embrace of a dead man—all that was left of your father." Nancy stopped short of revealing more of the news James had included in his last letter. He had made his decision. He would stand with the Union. An industrialist with military education, social position, practical skills, and political influence in Pennsylvania, he was considering a commission in what would be the Northern forces, should the conflict many predicted come to fruition. Not only might he suffer and die in battle, but he would wear the blue uniform of those who disrupted her sleep. The nightmares came only occasionally now, but, when they came, they were as sharp and painful as the day her life with David was torn away.

Tears coursed down Margaret's cheeks as she touched her mother's face. "I'm sorry, Mother. I won't bring all this up again. You have made our lives so good since I was born, I forget there was so much sadness before."

"I don't think about it as much as I once did. But, the thought of marrying again—of having a man's arms around me—well, it terrifies me. Now, that would be a fine way to start a marriage—*I love you, but I'd rather you not touch me!*"

Margaret smiled at her Mother's attempt at humor.

202

"Besides," Nancy raised her eyebrows and added, "James travels in social circles where an Indian woman might feel profoundly uncomfortable!"

The thunder of drums and blaring trumpets announced the imminent arrival of Stephen Douglas at the train station.

"Margaret, let's close up shop and go see what the Little Giant has to say. This might be a great day in history, and we would have missed it."

Margaret nodded and removed her apron.

* * * * * * * * *

The crowd was pressed into the lobby of the hotel, but Margaret and Nancy excused their way to the sidewalk. It occurred to Nancy that their Cherokee faces must be of advantage. Whether from shock or aversion, the mass of people seemed to part at their passage like the Red Sea under the inspired hand of Moses.

The women stood at the curb in time to witness the last of the bands, in all their brassy, clamorous brilliance, and to view the passing of the uniformed militia. With her first glimpse of the blue coats, Nancy's heart quickened and became heavy in her chest; the blood drained from her face. In panic, she had an urge to seize her daughter and to return to the safety of the shop. Perspiration erupted from Nancy's brow, and her head seemed heavy. The sidewalk rolled under her feet.

"Mother!" Margaret exclaimed, as Nancy's body slumped against her shoulder.

"Mrs. Hilderbrand!" cried a familiar voice.

A strong grip was on her forearm, and a sturdy support held her at the shoulders. Nancy looked up into the concerned face of Thomas, the deliveryman.

"Oh, Thomas," Nancy gasped. "Thank you! I don't know what's come over me. I feel faint."

"Let's get her out of this crowd, Margaret," said Thomas. "She needs to lie down."

Working their return through the throng, Thomas and Margaret entered the lobby, where Thomas said, "Excuse my being forward, Mrs. Hilderbrand," then gathered Nancy up in his arms like a child. He carried her back to the storefront, where Margaret unlocked the door and directed him to lay Nancy on the settee.

"Thank you," Nancy whispered, as she rested her head on the arm cushion. "I don't know what came over me."

"Miss Margaret, you want me to go get a doctor?" asked Thomas.

"No, Thomas—" Nancy began.

"Yes, please, Thomas—thank you," Margaret interrupted.

Nancy was too tired to muster the strength to argue with her daughter.

Margaret and Thomas waited in the hallway outside the shop, where the front curtains had been drawn for privacy.

Margaret's concern for her mother outweighed awareness that she was in the company of the man who earlier had been the object of such interest. "I have never known Mother to be ill—not once. At least, she has never given any indication."

"The crowd was a might oppressive," offered Thomas.

Margaret nodded, as she leaned against the wall and nibbled the knuckle of her forefinger.

The shop door opened, and the doctor directed, "You may come in now."

Margaret moved toward the door, but Thomas said, "I'll wait out here."

"Don't go, please," Margaret entreated.

"No, ma'am, I'll stay right here—in case you need me."

Margaret found Nancy sitting upright, her elbow on the arm of the settee, her head resting on her fingers. Nancy said nothing. Margaret knelt before her mother, took Nancy's hand, and pressed it between her own. She asked the doctor, "What's wrong?"

"Miss Hilderbrand, your mother needs rest. Her heart seems weak—it may be in the process of failing her."

"Her heart?" Margaret waited for the words to penetrate her understanding. "But Mother is so young!"

"Age really has little to do with it," replied the doctor. "Some hearts cannot take as much as others. Others, though strong, can only take so much." The doctor repacked his bag and snapped it shut, as he said, "I venture to say, your mother's heart has withstood more than its share in her relatively young life. She needs rest. She needs to slow down, reduce work and stress as much as possible. I want to see her in a week. In the meantime, please feel free to call for me." He made his way to the door, leaving the women to reflect on his diagnosis.

Margaret laid her head on Nancy's hand and wept.

"I'm sorry, Margaret. I would not want to worry you."

"I should not have upset you today."

"Maggie, no! The doctor said this episode has been coming for a time now." Nancy tried to laugh through her weariness. "I thought I was fainting at the sight of the bluecoats—thought maybe this old Indian ought to run for cover!"

Margaret was silent for a while, then looked at Nancy. "Mother, let's go home."

Nancy nodded. "Yes, I would like for you to be back with family." She looked around the shop, then rubbed her forehead. "I'll need to stay long enough to wrap up things here with Opal. I'll write Uncle Silas and Aunt Carol. We'll try to be home and settled in before the worst part of winter." Nancy looked toward the door. "Where did your young Mr. McNeal go? I need to thank him again."

"Oh, Thomas! He's waiting outside!" Margaret rushed to give him entrance.

Thomas, hesitant, approached the settee. "Are you feeling better, ma'am?"

"Just a little tired, Thomas," Nancy replied. "Thank you for your assistance today."

"My pleasure, ma'am. I hope you continue to improve."

"Thank you. I just need to get some rest. I've been working a bit too much."

"Can I see you home, ma'am?" he offered.

"Thank you, Thomas, for the offer, but I need to stay and wait for Mrs. Stevens to pick up her hat. Opal might not be back in time."

"No, Mother, you don't. Thomas, if you have time, please take Mother to the apartment. I'll stay here and see to Mrs. Stevens. Then I'll close up and follow."

"Be happy to, Miss Margaret."

"Margaret," she corrected.

Thomas smiled. "Yes, ma'am—Margaret. Mrs. Hilderbrand, are you ready? Are you able to walk, ma'am?"

"Oh, yes, Thomas! Embarrassment would finish me off, if you had to carry me home like a babe in arms." Nancy's laugh was weak. "We can go out the delivery entrance and be just a short distance from the apartment."

"Thomas, make her lie down," Margaret ordered, "and I'll be there as soon as I can."

As she waited for the arrival of Mrs. Stevens, Margaret busied herself about the shop. Inhaling deep, sighing breaths of air, she tried to still the fear constricting her throat. Her mother was young, vital, beautiful—how could her heart be failing her? But, then, her heart had endured so much. Her mother, like Opal, had toiled—long, tireless hours, to stake her claim in the new world of the whites and to establish her presence as a woman to be admired and respected, regardless of the color of her skin. And, as she labored, ever challenging herself with new goals, Nancy carried the memory of David in her heart—there it lay, a smoldering ember.

Margaret sat on the stool in the workroom and held her head in her hands. How could she have persisted in her nagging about James Dunwoody? How could she have infringed on this part of her mother that was so private, so personal—that carried with it the potential for such pain?

Margaret's tears made spots on the fold of silk remnant on which they fell.

* * * * * * * * * *

"Thomas, I'll just sit here for a while and put my feet up." Nancy lowered herself to the armchair and raised her feet to the fringed ottoman. "Don't let me keep you from your work. I have taken too much of your time already."

"Oh, no problem, ma'am. I'm finished for the day. I was just enjoying the hubbub when I saw you and Margaret making your way to the street. I'm glad I was nearby when you fell ill."

"So am I." Nancy smoothed her hair back from her face. "I cannot believe this has happened to me! I can't remember ever feeling poorly—except when Maggie was born—and that was only natural." Nancy looked around the apartment as if she were taking in her surroundings for the first time. "I have never been unable to do whatever I put my mind to doing—now, suddenly, I feel as weak as a new kitten!"

"Maybe you'll feel better with some rest," he suggested.

Nancy said, "Thomas, please sit and visit with me for a bit, would you?" She gestured toward the matching armchair opposite her.

"It would be a pleasure, ma'am." He hesitated, before sitting. "Could I get you something? Fix you some tea?"

"That would be very nice, Thomas. There is a burner on the counter next to the sink—around there," she pointed to the corner just past the tall bookcase facing their chairs. "The tea and sugar are on the shelf above, and the milk is in the ice box."

Thomas made comforting, bustling noises in the tiny kitchen. Nancy smiled at her mental picture of his tall, lanky form maneuvering about the area. She liked this young man. Margaret was correct in her assessment of his good looks—black hair that glistened with copper highlights in the late afternoon sun streaming from the sole window in the parlor, deep blue eyes that sparkled with health and humor, fair skin with a cast of dark stubble, and cheeks that tended to ruddiness.

"Thomas how long have you been in this country?" Nancy questioned.

"Nigh on to a fortnight, ma'am."

"How are you liking your new home?"

"Well, I've been busy. My uncle put me to work about as soon as I arrived here. Guess he figured he'd keep me out of trouble that way," he laughed. "I miss Scotland, but I figure a man can be happy anywhere if he puts his mind to it."

"Your uncle must care about you very much—to bring you here, arrange for a job for you."

"Yes, he's been concerned about my mother and me, since my father, his brother, died when I was ten. Cream and sugar?" he asked.

"Yes, please."

He brought in two saucers holding steaming cups of tea. He set one on the table at Nancy's side. The other he held while he lowered himself to the armchair, leaned back, and crossed his long legs. "We had a bit of acreage. Mom and I had enough, especially when I began working at the iron factory, but my uncle always kept in touch and made sure we lacked for nothing."

"What brought you to this country?" she inquired.

"Mom died last year."

"Oh, I'm sorry, Thomas."

"Thank you, ma'am. Mom developed a morbid growth inside her. She went fast. Death was a blessed end to terrible pain."

She detected a tremor in his voice.

"My uncle had come already to this land of promise, and he used all his persuasiveness to encourage me to join him—to the point of paying my passage. So, here I am."

"And today," declared Nancy, "I am very glad you are here!"

"Well, Mrs. Hilderbrand, today, I myself am very glad I'm here." He saluted her with his cup.

They sipped their tea in silence, until Nancy asked, "Thomas, when do you begin at the ironworks?"

"Well, they're calling up men as they need them according to the waiting list—maybe a week or two."

Nancy noticed her hand was shaking as she placed her cup and saucer back on the table before speaking. "Thomas, I have a proposition. I am going to need a great deal of help in the next couple of months, to get ready for our move back to our home. I have orders to complete, packing to do, business affairs to see to. Margaret is a tremendous help—when she has time. But she also will be busy with her pupils and making arrangements for them after she is gone. Could I hire you for two months to help me in your extra time?"

"Well, ma'am, I don't know—I reckon that would work out."

"I would match what you are making now—that would double your income for several weeks," Nancy pointed out.

"That's mighty generous, ma'am. But the ironworks might call me up before then."

"Are you set on working at the foundry?"

"Like I told you, ma'am, I'm a farmer, not a foundry man. But the ironworks is the means to the end."

Nancy's voice grew stronger. She leaned forward. "I have access to land along the river—beautiful bottom land, dark and rich. You hold off on the ironworks for two months, and I might be able to get you a deal you can afford on some of that land—without ever going to the ironworks."

"Ma'am...I don't know...I—"

"Thomas, just two months. I plan to be home by the first of the year. I won't need your services after that."

211

"Well, my uncle may have my head for agreeing—he got me on the list at the foundry—but—all right, ma'am, two months. I'll come by your shop directly after my deliveries and hotel chores are done. I promise to be a good worker for you—I've never been afraid of hard work."

Nancy smiled and picked up her tea. "I have no doubt about it, Thomas."

Holding up her skirt, Margaret took the stairs two at a time. Bursting through the door, she halted at the sight of her mother and Thomas—lounging in the armchairs, sipping tea as if no crisis had ever transpired.

"Well, hello, Margaret!" Nancy greeted her daughter.

"Mother? Are you feeling better? Shouldn't you be lying down?"

"I am very tired, but I wanted to visit with Thomas for a bit. Now, I think I will go lie down." Nancy rose to her feet, and Thomas scurried to assist her. "Thank you, Thomas, but I think the floor has stopped rolling under me—at last."

"I'll help you, Mother," Margaret said, taking Nancy's arm. "You just need to get dressed for bed and rest."

"Yes, I will let you help me. Then, I want to thank Thomas for all his assistance this afternoon. You get some money from my purse, and you and Thomas go out and bring back a nice meal— enough for four. When Opal returns, we'll all have supper together. Will you accept our invitation to dinner, Mr. McNeal?"

"Why, yes, ma'am, I'd like that."

"Good," Nancy said over her shoulder, as she moved toward the bedroom. "Won't find that in your book of etiquette, will you, Maggie? Inviting a friend to dinner, but sending him out to buy it first?"

Margaret helped Nancy change into her nightdress. She knew, had her mother been feeling well, she would never have allowed Margaret's assistance. A gnawing fear intensified within her, as she held back tears by busying herself—putting away her mother's clothes in the wardrobe, straightening the covers, setting things in order on the bedside table.

Margaret had fluffed the pillow behind Nancy's head, when Nancy seized her wrist and said, "Enough, child. I plan to have a few good years ahead of me. Let me rest."

Margaret sat on the bed beside Nancy. "Mother, I am so afraid. I don't want to lose you."

"Well, Margaret, you will—at some point, you will. We must both take whatever days or months or years we have and make them good ones. Now, go on—let me have some quiet time before dinner. If you'll hand me my book on the dresser, I'll read for a bit and then take a nap."

Margaret handed Nancy the Stowe book she had been reading. "I'll be just outside if you need me."

Margaret thought there was a sallow caste to her mother's soft, tanned complexion, and the sparkle in her deep brown eyes was shaded by heavy, tired lids. Nancy looked so fragile, her form hardly making a ripple in the coverlet of the bed. Her face was still beautiful, framed by loose wisps of black hair; the only wrinkles were those where smiles had creased the corners of her eyes and mouth.

"You and Thomas decide on our dinner and then go and get whatever we need. Opal will be back before long, and, in the meantime, I will just be here resting. No need for you to sit there on guard."

"Are you sure?"

"Margaret, you are wearying me! Do as I say. I am not going anywhere, and there is nothing you can do for me. I want you to prepare dinner for four. Scat!"

"All right, Mother." Margaret closed the door partway, then opened it. "I love you, Mother."

"I love you, too, Maggie."

The door began to close.

Nancy called, "Maggie?"

"Yes, ma'am?"

"Get whatever you want for dinner, but for dessert let's have the chocolate cake encrusted with pecans from the hotel dining room." Nancy winked at Margaret.

Margaret laughed. "All right, Mother." The door shut, and Nancy closed her eyes.

Margaret entered the parlor to see Thomas coming from the kitchen with a cup of tea he extended toward her. "Cream and sugar?" he asked.

"Yes, thank you." She sat in the place her mother had vacated.

"I figured you might take it as your mother does." He took his seat again.

"How did she seem to you?" Margaret asked.

"She is not well, but she is in good spirits," he responded.

"I must get her back home—away from work, back with family."

"We will." He grinned. "Your mother has hired me to help her do just that."

Nancy's eyes flew open. "She has what?"

"Hired me—to help her wrap up her work here and to get her moved. She said you'd be busy seeing to your students, making preparations for them, and she wants to get moved by the New Year. So, she hired me to come to work after my regular hours with the hotel."

Margaret was confused. What had come over her mother? Was she not thinking clearly? "Thomas, we live very simply, and Mother is frugal—at her most extravagant! We have few belongings. I really don't know how much work there will be for you." She frowned. "I fear mother has been affected by this attack and is not thinking clearly."

His smile was sympathetic yet reassuring. "Oh, I think she is still as clever as she is beautiful." He looked at the clock on the bookcase. "Hadn't we been getting our dinner, as your mother directed? Opal will be back before long, and we will all be ready to eat."

* * * * * * * * *

Nancy was dozing, when she heard Opal open the door and call her name.

"In here!" she answered.

Opal, alarm clouding her face, entered the bedroom. Coming to her side, she asked, "Nancy, what has happened? I got back to the shop and it was closed. McNeal said his nephew had brought you home sick."

"I fainted—had some sort of attack. Margaret had Thomas call the doctor. It seems I have a weak heart."

Opal sat on the bed. "No, Nancy! What does it mean?"

"The doctor says I have to rest—slow down, less work, take it easy."

"He must not know you very well!"

"No—but I think he's right, Opal. I do feel very weak after the spell today. I'm sure with rest I'll feel better, but this has shaken me up. And Margaret has fussed till I just made her leave," she laughed, "with the handsome deliveryman!"

"No! Well, leave it to Mama to get her daughter anything she wants—even if it means using a bad heart to get her girl a man!" A sob escaped Opal, as her jesting turned to tears.

"Opal, no, please don't!" begged Nancy.

Opal shook her head and sighed, fending off the onslaught of misery. "Nancy, the thought of losing you cuts me to the core. You have been more than my partner—you have been my friend."

"And you have been the same to me." Nancy's agreement was soft, earnest. "I never would have stood a chance in this place, had you not taken me in, given me a job and a place to live."

Opal laughed and clasped Nancy's hand. Holding it up between them, she declared, "Well, there be a shade or two difference in the color of our skin, but we're shoulder to shoulder in this life. And we're making it, girl, we're making it!"

Nancy laughed as she brought Opal's warm brown hand to her lips. "Thank you, Opal."

Opal released her grip and patted Nancy's arm. "Now, do you feel like eating something?"

"No, not really. But don't you bother about supper. I sent Thomas and Margaret out to get dinner for us. They should be coming back soon."

"I say, you do move fast!"

Nancy laid her hand on Opal's. "Opal, we're going back home in a couple of months. I want Maggie near family. I'll try to get my orders finished before I go, but I won't be taking any new ones."

Opal covered Nancy's hand with her own. "I understand. I'll keep L & H going with my hats, and if you ever feel like coming back—or maybe get to where you would want to take orders and work at home, like we talked about—you just let me know."

"Thank you, Opal. You are a dear friend. I can never thank you for all you have done for us."

"Don't get into all that kind of stuff," she said, rising to her feet. She went toward the door, then turned to add, "No need to thank me—we're friends. I love you like a sister." She hid the tears in her eyes as she shut the door behind her.

Margaret was so eager to return to her mother, she could not relish the time alone with Thomas. "Maybe we could just ask your uncle to place an order for us with the cook at the hotel. Mother wanted to get the chocolate cake with pecans from there—we might as well get everything in one place."

"Whatever you think your mother would like," Thomas agreed.

Mr. McNeal was setting mail and messages in their appropriate cubbyholes as Margaret and Thomas approached.

"Hello, Uncle!"

Mr. McNeal looked over his shoulder. "Thomas! Just a shake." He delivered three more envelopes, then gave them his attention. "Miss Hilderbrand," he greeted her. "How's your mother?"

"She's resting, thank you." Her voice quivered as she replied.

Mr. McNeal said, "Please give her my regards, and tell her I'll be praying for her."

Margaret was comforted by his choice of words. "Why—thank you, Mr. McNeal."

"Uncle, Mrs. Hilderbrand sent us to fetch dinner for four, and she specially requested the chocolate cake with pecans. Think you can place an order for us with the cook."

"No problem, son. Think four of today's specials will suffice—roast beef with vegetables?"

Thomas looked at Margaret. "Sounds good to me—what about you?"

Margaret said, "That's fine."

"Just have a seat, and I'll have a waiter bring it out when it's ready." Mr. McNeal wrote the order on a slip of paper, then motioned for a porter to take it to the kitchen.

"Let's sit over here." James motioned to a padded bench at the rear of the lobby, where a large, multi-paned window looked out on a courtyard set with planters of evergreens interwoven among cobblestone walkways. In nooks here and there, pots of fall flowers punctuated the serenity of the garden with eruptions of fiery colors.

"Your mother is a true lady," Thomas commented. "I trust she will be better soon."

"I hope so," replied Margaret. "I have never seen my mother ill. It was a shock to see her so fragile today."

"Fragile in body, perhaps, but I venture to say she is a woman of strong mind and character."

"Oh, yes—very. She has a backbone of steel and has endured so much. Of course, that was before I was born—for the most part." Margaret avoided Thomas's gaze and tried to focus her clouding eyes on the garden before her.

"Margaret? Margaret, look at me. Are you crying? Please, don't cry. I'm sure your mother will improve."

"I'm afraid I caused it."

"What? Your mother's attack? Oh, no, Margaret, you couldn't have caused it."

"But I believe I did. I was trying to persuade Mother to consider marrying again. I want her to be happy, and I thought her friend, Mr. Dunwoody, could make her happy. It upset her. I know it did."

"Margaret, it would upset her even more to know you thought this. She would be the first to assure you, you are wrong."

Margaret's eyes were red, and her cheeks were wet with unchecked tears, as she faced him. "I don't want her to die, Thomas."

"Maggie, we'll take good care of her." He patted her hand and gave her a handkerchief from his hip pocket. "Your mother can't live forever—none of us can. But we can help her live well and content, whatever time she has."

"Thank you, Thomas." She smiled. "I am beginning to understand why my mother wanted to hire you."

* * * * * * * * * *

Margaret finished her last class and hurried to the shop, where, she trusted, she would find her mother and Thomas crating the sewing machine, fabric, and notions Opal had told Nancy to take—

just in case. Margaret was eager to be home for Christmas, but, at the same time, her heart ached to think of leaving Thomas. They had been fellow-soldiers in their campaign to care for Nancy and to see to her resettlement. Her mother seemed to be as important to Thomas as she was to her own daughter. Though it made Margaret's affection for him even stronger, she also found his relationship with her mother a bit unsettling. They seemed to share some special bond and confidences that excluded her, and, at times, she feared she might be jealous of her own mother. Nancy was considered an attractive woman, and she did seem to be happy and more vigorous in the presence of her strong, young hired hand.

The bell rang as Margaret entered the store. Mother and Thomas were sitting in the anteroom, and it seemed Margaret had interrupted Mother's reading of the letters in her hand.

"Well, something of interest in today's mail?" Margaret asked, as she removed her cloak and hung it on the hall tree.

"Yes, a couple of letters—one from Uncle Silas, the other from James. Sit down, Margaret," Nancy ordered.

Margaret sat in one of the floral stuffed chairs.

"I wrote to Silas some weeks ago—right after my little fainting spell. I told him we were coming home. I also told him I did not want to uproot Sara and Josiah from our house, especially with the children—and Silas and Carol need them nearby. Well, I asked Silas to find us some more land—I'd trust his judgment. Told him to have his men start building us a new house." She held up the letter. "Silas has written to tell me Josiah still had the land at Stanley, where he and Sara had planned to live. The site was already cleared, and the basic log structure still standing. He says Josiah and I can just swap and re-register deeds. He said he's had a crew devoted to our house and it will be ready in time for Christmas!" Tears filled Nancy's eyes. "I wanted it to be my present to you."

Margaret knelt at Nancy's feet. "Mother, it is the best present you could have ever given me. Thank you."

"I hope you're happy about it. Silas says its beautiful land—lies on both sides of the trail, about halfway up the mountain and down to the river. I know it's not within easy walking distance, but we'll be close enough to see the family on a regular basis."

"It sounds perfect. And, really, Mother, this way you will have more peace and quiet. I know you enjoy the grandchildren, but this way you won't be worn out by them every day."

Nancy glanced at Thomas, before continuing. "I'm so happy you are pleased. I know I am." She turned the other letter over to open it. "Well, let me see what James has written." She broke the seal and removed the folded sheet.

Margaret and Thomas waited while she read the letter.

Nancy looked stunned, then, spoke with hesitation, "James says South Carolina is on the verge of secession—he anticipates it before the end of the year. He says, if the mood of South Carolina is any indication, within months we will be in the middle of armed conflict." Nancy stopped reading. Silence prevailed until she regained her breath and spoke, "I hadn't told you, but James was offered a commission in the army of Pennsylvania—he has business and political ties there and, of course, the foundry. He is going to accept the commission. He states, 'Industrialization—not slave labor—is the future of our country. This is a fact with which even the agrarian south must come to terms.'"

"Well, hallelujah!" Opal had come around the screen in time to hear Nancy's reading.

Nancy continued, "I will be in Chattanooga by the middle of December. I look forward to seeing you then." Her eyes continued to scan the remainder of the page; then, hands quivering, she folded the paper and returned it to the envelope.

Margaret took the letters from Nancy's hand. "Mother, enough. Let's see about getting you home. You need to eat something and rest. You've had a long day."

"Margaret, if you don't stop fretting over me like an old mother hen, I declare, I'll be forced to wring your neck and fry you up for supper!"

Thomas teased, "Don't invite me to dinner—hen's a bit scrawny, if you ask me."

Opal whooped, as Nancy and Thomas laughed at Maggie's expense.

"And what makes you think you'd be invited to dinner anyway, McNeal!" Margaret retorted.

"Your mother has told me I have a standing invitation. The same goes for you—you may join your mother and me anytime you wish."

Opal chuckled again and went behind the screen, declaring, "This is more than I can stand—I got to get back to work! Nancy, let me know when you're ready."

"Ready for what?" asked Margaret.

"Ready to go to the apartment. Opal and I are closing up a bit early. We have some paperwork to go over this evening."

"What about supper?"

"We'll fix something."

"I'll go on and get something ready," Margaret countered, and she moved to retrieve her cape.

"No, Maggie! You are going out to dinner," her mother called to stop her.

"I am?"

"Yes, Thomas just asked me a while ago if I would mind his taking you out this evening."

"Well, did you or Thomas think about asking me if I wanted to go out this evening?"

Nancy and Thomas looked at each other.

"No," replied Nancy, smirking.

Thomas asked. "Would you like to go out to dinner with me this evening?"

"Oh, well, thank you for asking!" she mocked. "How kind of you!"

Nancy teased, "Oh, Thomas is kind—that he is."

Thomas stood and leaned over Nancy to take her hand. "Thank you, Mrs. Hilderbrand. I'll take good care of her." Margaret saw in

Thomas's face and heard in his voice a depth of affection that startled her.

Nancy looked at Thomas with eyes full of love, and Margaret wondered at the strange attachment to him her mother had developed. Margaret had allowed concern for her mother to overshadow her feelings for Thomas. She had determined there was no time for childish infatuation when her mother's state of health was so precarious. But while Margaret was trying to ignore and discount her own feelings for Thomas, she wondered if Nancy had stolen the heart of the only man Margaret had ever loved.

Thomas collected Margaret's wrap but threw it over his shoulder. "You won't be needing this," he said, "We're not going far."

He took her hand and tucked her arm under his. "Your table awaits, Miss Hilderbrand."

Margaret was silent as he led her down the hallway, lined with the glow of candelabras on gleaming cherry side tables, supporting vases of fresh flowers, and ensconced beside gilt-framed paintings of the local mountains and valleys in a variety of seasonal finery. Her mind awhirl, Thomas led her through the lobby, past klatches of business men, who were puffing smoke and spouting speculations about the economy and upcoming election, and their elegant wives, some dressed in her mother's handiwork and dripping honeyed tones of flattery from their rouged and pouty mouths.

Their processional ended at the entrance to the darkened, candlelit dining room. The head waiter met them at the door and said, "Mr. McNeal, I have your table ready." He escorted them to the garden nook, seated Margaret amid the luxuriant wrap of foliage, and announced with a rare smile, "Everything is prepared as you requested, sir."

"Thank you," Thomas replied. There seemed to be a sparkle of excitement in his mellow voice, and Margaret noticed his eyes crinkled at the corners. Turning to her, he commented, "You are unusually quiet."

"I—I never expected...I mean—"

"I never thought I'd see you at a loss for words!" She sensed his amusement was not at her expense but was delight over her complete surprise.

"You have had this planned!" she realized.

"For a while. You have been so consumed with your mother, you were smothering her and avoiding me. We had to get you out—give her a breather and give me some time with you alone."

"But, I thought—well, never mind."

"What? Finish."

"No, it's silly."

"Nothing about you is silly, Maggie." He took her hand and kissed it.

Margaret was breathless. "I—I thought it was mother you cared about."

"It is—I mean, I do. I love her, almost as much as you do, I would say. She will be the most wonderful mother-in-law any man ever had."

"What?"

"I said, she will make a wonderful mother-in-law. You will marry me, won't you?"

To Margaret it seemed the world fell silent. The low rumble of the patrons' voices; the percussive rhythms of moving, serving, dining, clearing; the gurgle and splash of the nearby waterfall—all was quiet, except the beating of her heart. All was still, except the pulsing at her temple.

"Look under your napkin." Thomas broke the silence and prodded her to action.

Margaret moved the crisp white linen. Under it rested a long red velvet box.

"Open it, Maggie."

Margaret was stunned, moving on command without thinking. She opened the lid. Resting on the satin lining of the container was a gold locket, covered with engraved vines and roses, centered by an inset heart of polished gold for inscription. "Thomas!" she whispered. She removed it from the box and laid its golden warmth in the palm of her hand.

"Read the words on the front." She heard his voice break.

"Forever begins." She was puzzled and looked at him for explanation.

Breathless, Thomas said, "Open it."

Inside the locket was engraved the date: "Dec. 20, 1860."

"That's the date I'd like for us to be married—if you will have me. I know that's not much time to plan a wedding, and I'm taking a chance you won't even have me. Maybe I should have waited on the locket. But, who knows what the future holds? If it's to be, I want our time together to begin right away—and with your mother's health…" Thomas seemed to run out of words.

Tears welled in her eyes.

Thomas waited while Margaret searched for words.

"I love you, Maggie." His declaration was tinged with anxiety, urgency.

Dark eyes awash with emotion, Margaret blinked away the clouds and whispered, "I love you, too, Thomas." Her gaze locked on his clear blue eyes. "And, yes, I will marry you—I will have you, forever."

Thomas took her hands in his and held them to his lips. Tears glistened on his own cheeks, as he exhaled. "Oh, Maggie, I was so afraid you would refuse me. I'm not wealthy or handsome, but I'm strong—a hard worker. I'll give you every day of my life—to make you happy, to care for you, to be a good husband, a good father to our children someday."

Margaret laughed through her tears. "Thomas, enough! I love you. I have no doubts." She questioned, "But how do you know what kind of wife I will be?"

"Ah, Maggie, I see your mother. You are your mother's daughter. Had your father survived, he would have been as proud and happy today as he was the day they married."

Thomas retrieved the locket from her hand and skirted the table to fasten the pendant around Maggie's neck. "Besides," he teased, "she assures me you are a fine cook, adequate housekeeper, and can sew on a button with the best of them." Glancing around the dining room, he leaned over and gave Maggie a sweet, slow kiss.

The waiter's clearing his throat interrupted them. "Excuse me, sir, miss."

Thomas traced the outline of her face with the back of his hand, as he moved to return to his seat.

"Miss Margaret Hilderbrand?"

"Yes?"

"These are for you." The man set a bouquet of russet and gold autumn flowers at Margaret's place.

"Oh, Thomas, they are beautiful!"

"They are, but I didn't order them! What does the card say?"

Margaret read the card and covered her mouth to quiet her laughter. "Bring dessert (chocolate cake with pecans) back to the apartment so we can talk about wedding plans. I'm so happy! Love, Mother."

December 20, 1860

The new house rested on a rise above the Tennessee, churning broad and deep at the foot of the slope. The main body of the house was the existing log structure, but new, framed ells extended to the east and to the south, facing the stream. Porches spanned the east and west sides and stretched across the back parallel to the river. A towering shade oak shadowed the front entrance and the western porch, where one might sit in view of the river trail and, leading from it, the graveled road to the front yard.

Lying in the cradle of the downy feather bed, Nancy opened her eyes and looked out the window over the dresser. The wedding day had dawned gray and cold; clouds billowed and puffed over the mountains. But, Nancy thought, a blanket of clean, white snow would only add to the beauty of this day.

She remembered her bags still stacked at the foot of the bed and reminded herself to hang her dress to let the wrinkles fall out. Margaret's dress—the gown Carol had worn when she married Silas, had been cleaned, freshly pressed, and laid on the trunk in the other bedroom, the larger of the two, which would be shared by Margaret and Thomas.

Nancy had been concerned that there was no time to make a special wedding dress for her daughter; but Margaret had been thrilled when Carol, saying she would always consider herself Maggie's second mother, offered hers as her wedding gift. Though a bit old-fashioned, Nancy thought, it was still like new and needed only a tuck here and there for a perfect fit. And, she thought, if a wedding dress could be a good luck charm and bring with it the same happiness known to Silas and Carol, then the future looked bright for the McNeals.

Nancy willed herself to get up and start the day. Carol and Sara would be arriving soon, bringing with them ham and biscuits for breakfast and the major portion of the meal for the reception. Nancy would start a pot of coffee on the wood stove and have it ready when they arrived. Then, she, Carol, and Opal would prepare the celebration table, while Sara helped Margaret with her bridal preparation.

The guests would begin arriving by ten for the wedding at eleven. The weekend preacher, who held services at the schoolhouse, had stayed over to perform the ceremony. The Andersons were coming from Chattanooga, with Lily, her husband, and the new baby. Josiah would bring Thomas, Silas, and the children—Samuel, Clara, and Tillie. The wedding would be immediate family and friends, but Nancy still anticipated a joyful, boisterous celebration.

Nancy wrapped her robe around her, cushioned her feet in heavy woolen socks, and entered the open doorway to the kitchen. The stove was already warming the open space, and the smell of coffee beckoned. Margaret, peering out the front window, was huddled beside it on a chair. She was still in her flannel nightdress, with her feet in the seat, her arms encircling her legs. She looked so young, beautiful, and innocent, Nancy had to fight back tears. "Good morning! I thought the bride might sleep late this morning."

Margaret's smile was gentle. "Good morning, Mother. I slept hard for a while, but then woke up early and couldn't go back to sleep."

"Nerves?" asked Nancy.

"Not really," replied Margaret. "Just thinking about everything that has happened."

"We have had some major life changes in the past two or three months!"

"Yes, but I feel at peace here—content. It's good to be home to stay."

"I'm glad you feel that way. I'm also glad you've got a fire going and coffee ready." Nancy rubbed her hands together and then reached for a cup from the shelf above the sink.

"Go ahead and grab another of those, if you don't mind. I'm chilled to the bone!" Opal entered from the parlor between the eat-in kitchen and Maggie's bedroom. She was covered, head to toe, in her blanket.

Margaret laughed. "Opal, you look like an old Indian on a cold day. How did you sleep?"

"That day bed sleeps good! Had the best sleep I've had in ages! It's waking up in this cold that's not going well."

Nancy handed her the cup. "Here, bundle up next to the stove and drink this."

Opal seated herself opposite Margaret, and Nancy pulled up a third chair to join them.

"Well, we're a fine bunch, aren't we?" Opal observed. "The Indian princess, the mother of the bride, and one frozen black woman, huddled around this pot-bellied stove as if it were just any old day in winter."

Their laughter chugged to a halt with Nancy's admonition, "We'd best not be lounging here when Carol arrives. The schoolmarm will give us a tongue-lashing and warm up the seats of our pants."

"Well, right now, I'd be pleased to have her warm up mine!" declared Opal, again setting them off in gales of mirth.

Sara coiled Margaret's hair into a bun and pinned it in the white lace netting. She placed the pale blue and white satin headpiece—Opal's wedding gift, on Maggie's head and arranged the ribbons trailing from pearl-centered rosettes at the back. "You look so beautiful, Maggie. I can't believe you're all grown up and getting married!"

"Thank you, Sara," Margaret exhaled, as she gave her sister a hug. "Will you get Mother for me now?"

Sara nodded and went to find Nancy, who was at the center of a bevy of guests. Sara noted the Andersons with Thomas's uncle. Making a quick mental checklist, she scanned the room and concluded everyone had arrived. She saw Josiah holding Tillie at the far entrance to the other bedroom. Catching his attention, she signed to ask if Thomas was ready. Josiah peeked into the bedroom behind him, then turned to grin and raised his thumb.

Sara saw Uncle Silas, sitting in his chair by the stove, with Samuel hanging over his shoulder and Clara on his lap. He was entertaining them with his coin tricks. *As usual*, she thought, *we can count on Uncle Silas to keep the children occupied.*

Sara got Nancy's attention and beckoned her with her finger. Nancy started toward the bedroom, when someone called out, "James!"

Nancy whirled toward the voice and then looked to the door. "James!" she cried. Scurrying as fast as she could through the assemblage of hoops and crinolines, she made her way to her friend's embrace.

"Do you mind an uninvited guest showing up like this?" he asked.

"Oh, no," Nancy replied, "Never uninvited—just unexpected! But what a wonderful surprise!"

"I am sorry not to tell you in advance. I got held up and couldn't make it by the middle of the month as I said; then it was too late to get a letter to you to let you know I would be here by Christmas."

Charlotte and Lily had made their way to greet James, so Nancy said, "I must leave now and see to Maggie. We'll talk later when we have more time."

James gave her a kiss on the cheek, held her gaze, and said, "Yes, later."

Nancy followed Sara into the bedroom, where Margaret stood; and Nancy was as moved as she had been the morning Carol laid her newborn daughter in her arms. Nancy cupped her hands over her mouth and nose and choked on her sobs.

"Oh, Mother, please, don't—you'll get your eyes all red!"

Nancy sat in the chair before the vanity table and heaved a deep sigh.

Sara came to Margaret's side and took her hand. "I need to see to the children. I love you, Maggie. Be happy." She kissed her sister and left the room.

"Are you all right, Mother? I hope this day isn't going to be too trying for you."

"Oh, Maggie, I'm just so happy! This day is going to be wonderful! Thomas is a good man, who loves you with all his heart. He will take care of you and be a good father to your children. What more could any mother hope?"

Margaret reached into the drawer of the vanity table. "I almost forgot." She held up the beaded purse. "I want to carry this today."

Nancy took the leather bag from her daughter's hand. "I remember the day your father gave it to me—our wedding day. I thought it was so beautiful—because I saw it through the eyes of love." She handed it back. "Love is the greatest gift, Maggie. It brings tremendous joy, but it also can help us through the worst of storms. They will come—as surely as the sun rises in the eastern sky, they will come. But you and Thomas love each other. Reach out and hold tight to each other, especially when the strong winds blow."

Margaret leaned over to kiss her mother. "I love you."

"I love you too, Maggie. Nancy's hands moved to the back of her neck. "I have something for you." Pulling the thong with the ring from her bodice, she handed it to Margaret. "This was your father's. I have worn it all these years. Now, I want you to have it—to give to your husband, if you wish."

"But, Mother—"

"No, it's yours. I have thought a great deal about many things in the last couple of months. I have used work to avoid dealing with the past and moving into the future. Now, I cannot work, and I realize I must live in the present and cherish each day as it comes."

Margaret dropped the leather strip with the golden band into the deerskin purse. "I'm glad, Mother. I know we'll be happy."

"Yes, I believe we will. Now, give your old mother a hand up. I want to go see my son."

Nancy stopped in the parlor, retrieved an envelope from the bureau, and placed it under her arm. Gathering her skirt close to her and stealing around the crowd to the doorway where Josiah stood guard, she asked, with a grin, "May I have permission to go in and see Thomas?"

Josiah turned to assess the situation in the room and then stepped aside. "I think he's presentable—permission granted."

"Mrs. Hilderbrand! Come in and take one last look before the bridegroom melts right into the floor!" Thomas's face was flushed crimson, and perspiration rolled down his cheeks.

"I'll leave you two to talk," offered Mr. McNeal, patting his nephew's shoulder and nodding to Nancy as he passed to the kitchen.

"Thomas McNeal!" she exclaimed. "Had this wedding been in summer, you'd be nothing but a puddle by now!"

Thomas mopped his brow. "I'm sorry, Mrs. Hilderbrand. I don't know what's come over me! I'm marrying the woman I love." He smiled at her and raised his eyebrows. "One of the two most beautiful women in the country. And look at me!" He held out his trembling hands for her to view.

Nancy took his hands, pulled him to the edge of the bed, and said, "Sit, relax for a minute." When he had settled, she continued, "Thomas, I have a wedding gift for you." She took a document from the envelope and handed it to him. "It's the deed to this property—made out in the names of 'Mr. and Mrs. Thomas McNeal.'"

"But, Mrs. Hilderbrand, this is your home!"

"No, this is your home," she countered. "Oh, of course, I expect to have a bed available to me when I come to visit my grandchildren. But this home is yours and Maggie's. I expect to see a barn and garden and livestock come next spring. You take that money you saved up and see to it."

"Mrs. Hilderbrand, I don't know what to say—"

"For one thing, say, 'Nancy'—saves time."

"Nancy, thank you." Thomas's eyes grew misty. He held her hand. "Next to Margaret and my mother, I love you more than any woman I have ever known."

Nancy patted his hand. "I love you too, son." She teased, "And you've got your women in just the right order! Now, put that deed in your pocket, and you can show it to Margaret later."

"Yes, ma'am."

"Are you still planning on staying here for your honeymoon?" she asked as she moved toward the door.

"Yes, ma'am, we thought we would."

"Well, good! Your first night in your new home! Charlotte has asked me to come for a visit, so I'll be going back in town with them and Opal." Nancy looked at the clock on the dresser, then ordered, "Up and ready, Thomas! It's time!"

She glanced back and smiled to see Thomas place the deed in his pocket, take a deep breath, and wipe his brow one more time.

It was nearly three before the convoy to Chattanooga left; the carriage with the Andersons and Opal, Mr. McNeal riding his horse alongside, and James's buggy moved eastward on the trail toward Chattanooga. Nancy waved at Thomas and Margaret McNeal, standing on the porch of their new home, arms wrapped around each other. Nancy was tired, but overjoyed—Maggie was home, happy, and in the embrace of a husband whose love would sustain her through the blessings and trials of life. Content, at peace, and comfortably ensconced in a woolen cloak and lap blanket, Nancy settled herself in the plush leather corner of the buggy seat. Her eyes caught sight of James's loving gaze, then closed under the weight of weariness.

* * * * * * * * *

Margaret and Thomas remained embraced as they entered the warmth of the kitchen. The house, scrubbed and set in order by Aunt Carol, Opal and Sara, seemed to echo with the voices and sounds of celebration. The oval dining table in the center of the room had been laid with a fresh linen cloth, and the remaining food covered. The opened wedding gifts had been arranged on the sideboard for reviewing in their quiet, private moments together.

"I have something to show you, Maggie." Thomas reached into his pocket and extracted the folded deed. "Your mother's gift to us."

Margaret took the paper, unfolded it, and scanned the page. "Our house?"

"She said for me to use our money for a barn and livestock—said she wants to see this farm settled come next spring."

"You mean she's not coming back till spring?"

"Why, I don't know. I guess I didn't understand it that way." Thomas took the deed, refolded it, and placed it with the packages on the sideboard. "I did get one thing clear—she said she expects to have her own bed available when she comes to visit her grandchildren." Thomas swooped down and caught Margaret up in his arms.

"Thomas!" she cried. "What are you doing?"

Thomas didn't respond, but raced across the kitchen, out the door to the porch, and down the steps, where he wheeled, retraced his steps, and ran back into the kitchen, kicking the door closed behind him.

Taking a deep breath, he panted, "Had to carry the bride across the threshold of her new home! Now, it's all proper!"

"Thomas McNeal, you're a wee bit daft," she mocked.

"Ah ha!" he cried and ran through the parlor entrance, across the sitting room, and into their bedroom. Throwing her on the middle of the bed, he declared, "And, you're a wee bit heavy!"

Margaret slipped from the cradle of Thomas's arms and reached for her robe.

Opening his eyes, Thomas whispered, "Don't leave."

"Just a moment. I have something for you." She sought the deerskin purse under the confusion of crinoline on the vanity table and returned to sit cross-legged next to her husband. He put his arm behind his head to prop himself up on the pillow.

She took the strip of leather from the pouch and removed the gold band. "This belonged to my father. Mother has worn it since he died. She gave it to me this morning. She thought I might want to give it to you. Do you think you would want to wear it?"

Thomas sat up and took the ring. He held it, considered it, and then replied, "I would be honored." He tried the ring on his finger, and it slid over his knuckle. He looked at the band. "Maggie, do you realize the love and the history this ring could speak—if only it had words?"

* * * * * * * * *

They were nearly to Chattanooga when Nancy woke with her mind whirling with the events of the day, punctuated by awareness—and some apprehension—that the question her friend had posed in his letter, surely, would surface again, this time face-to-face. She had not revealed the complete contents of the letter to her daughter; she had to have time to think without pressure, to sort through the emotions—the pleasure and pain of yesterday's memories, the possibilities of any tomorrows she might have. She was filled with joy and hope for Margaret's happiness, for her contentment with a good man who loved her, for the promise of the future that would be theirs. Could she—should she, dare consider a future with some of that same hope and promise?

James was, first and foremost, a good man. She knew he loved her, and she knew she loved him—surely, not with the intensity of youth with which she loved David. But, she knew her love for James was deep, rooted in friendship and the deep rich soil of age and experience. How much time might they have—who could say? What if war came—civil war, within the nation, between friends and brothers? How terrible even to contemplate—surely, on a par with the Removal in its cruelty, but this time crossing all barriers—North, South, black, white, slave, free, family against family—the whole country at odds and killing one another—until, perhaps, the Giver could no longer countenance the killing, the death and dying.

She might lose James also, and the thought made her shudder. But, she determined, worse than losing him, worse than the nightmares that might plague her at times, was the thought of losing him without giving either of them an opportunity for some peace and contentment—some joy, together.

"It was a nice wedding, don't you think, James?"

"You're back with me, I see." His words were soft through a gentle smile. "It was beautiful—simple, sweet, perfect. You ladies did a fine job of pulling things together on short notice. But, I fear, you may have overtaxed yourself."

"Oh, I'm a bit tired, but I'll be fine—and it was wonderful seeing Margaret so happy and to know she's settled in her own home with a good man like Thomas."

"And they should be safe and secure there when conflict comes," he added.

"Will it come to that, James?"

"It will. I don't want to disrupt the mood of the day, but I received a telegram this morning from an associate in Charleston. The Ordinance of Secession has been drafted and will be adopted today—South Carolina is declaring its independence."

"What does it all mean for you, now that you've accepted the commission?"

"I'll await orders and report to my duty post in a few weeks. Of course, I will be dealing with foundries supplying materials, but more than that I don't know yet."

The noise of the city street interrupted Nancy's thoughtful silence as the buggy stopped in front of the hotel. A porter came to take the bags and another to see to the buggy, as James helped Nancy to the ground.

"Why don't you go up to Charlotte's quarters, and I'll see to having a late supper brought up for all of us? Opal is going to join us. We'll have another private little celebration of our own and try to put all this secession business out of mind."

Nancy made her way up the stairs. Her feet were heavy. It had been a tiring day, full of plans that had come together and muddled thoughts that now were beginning to clear. Perhaps the energy to move her into a new path was not as forceful as it once was, but the determination to move could be just as strong. She was not—could not be—the woman she once was, but she was still Nancy Hilderbrand, older and wiser. If she had learned anything, it was the preciousness of time, in any quantity, with loved ones—and the futility and foolishness of losing the present in hopeless dreams and desires of the past.

Nancy sat on the top step at the landing. She smiled at the clarity and perception that had emerged through her weariness—she felt flushed. Maybe she was just a bit giddy after all the excitement.

"Nancy, are you all right?" James took the stairs two at a time to kneel before her and take her hands. "Do I need to call for the doctor?"

"No, no, James. I'm fine. Just a little tired and winded from the stairs."

"Please, Nancy, you would tell me, honestly?"

Nancy saw before her the man with whom she wanted to share whatever precious time there was—for either of them. Would there be fears and unhappy times? Maybe. Likely. But they would be overshadowed by the joy of togetherness and lessened by the blessedness of sharing.

"Oh, James…my dear James." She took a deep breath. "In your last letter, you put forth a proposition…"

"Yes, and I meant every word of the sentiment and the proposal."

"You see before you a woman who is a bit worn for her years …"

"No, I see—"

"But if the offer still stands, I accept."

"You accept?"

"Yes, James, I accept."

"Oh, Nancy, I have waited so long." He held her close, declaring, "I think I've loved you from the first time I saw you in the lobby with that stack of boxes."

"James, I'm sorry I have taken so long to clear the clouds from my mind. You are getting much less than the woman I was then."

James scooped her up in his arms and steadied her on her feet. "That will make it easier to get you upstairs if I have to carry you. This now, surely, will be another celebration!"

* * * * * * * * *

Margaret was clearing their lunch dishes, when the sound of a horse's canter urged her to the window. "Thomas, it's Josiah!"

Thomas rose from his seat and met Josiah at the porch. "Come in, Josiah. You're our first guest."

Josiah hitched his horse to the post and mounted the steps. "Good afternoon, Thomas," he greeted, shaking Thomas's hand. He entered the warmth of the kitchen and moved toward the stove, where he extended his palms over the rising heat. "Good to see you, Maggie. You've got things looking really nice here."

"Thanks. Good to see you, Josiah. What brings you all this way?" she asked.

Reaching into the right pocket of his coat, he pulled out an envelope and handed it to Margaret. "You got a letter from Nancy. Came by riverboat just this morning. We figured it might be important." From his other pocket he retrieved a pamphlet. "Here's a seed catalog for you, Thomas. Pa thought you might like to see it."

"Thanks, Josiah," replied Thomas, as he took the catalog, but waited for Maggie to read the letter.

Sitting in the chair by the stove, with daylight over her shoulder, Maggie read aloud:

January 10, 1861

> *Dear Thomas and Margaret,*
>
> *We know your new home is filled with love and happiness—and, we trust, warmth on these cold winter days. We hope and pray your life together will be richly blessed. Remember, never take each other for granted in the good times—and, in the bad times, fight shoulder to shoulder, not face to face.*
>
> *We are having a wonderful time—delicious food, concerts, the latest fashions! And the people here seem to be enjoying the sight of a stylish Indian woman squired by a dashing white gentleman.*
>
> *We soon will go on to Philadelphia, where James will see to business. The foundries must be ready to increase production, should matters in the country worsen. When he reports to his post, I will return to Chattanooga by train, first to Nashville, then to Chattanooga. James promises I will be treated royally. I am excited and just a bit anxious about the new experience, but I so look forward to seeing you, the barn, the garden, the cows, etc. Until then—*
>
> *We love you so very much.*

Your stepfather and mother, James and Nancy Dunwoody

Married Cincinnati, Ohio, Jan. 5, 1861

P. S. to Maggie

No fears, no tears, save those of happiness!

—Mother

* * * * * * * * *

April 13, 1861

Dear Thomas and Margaret,

By the time you receive this letter, I will be on my journey home. Any anxiety about my new adventure of train travel is far exceeded by concern over the events that transpired yesterday at Fort Sumter. James received a wire from Charlotte. William is sending the family to Chattanooga, at least temporarily. He and James agree we most certainly will be in a conflict such as never known to man. They feel Chattanooga will be a safer location, at least for the foreseen future.

I will meet Charlotte at her hotel suite and remain there to rest a few days. We will hire a carriage to transport us to your house on the river—perhaps, next week, Thursday or Friday, about mid-morning. Charlotte will return to the hotel. If you don't mind, my stay with you will be open-ended, depending on the unknown events ahead of us.

I know you will be concerned for my safety until I am tucked away in that soft bed you have waiting for me. Please, pray for our dear James—and for all those who will be involved in the terrible struggle that lies ahead.

With all my love, dear children,

—Mother

October 1862

Margaret was flushed and tired—but happy, contented, and, empty-armed, swaying in the rocker that had lulled her fussy daughter to sleep. The last of the family had left, Nancy was resting in her bed nook, and Thomas had gone out to feed and water the livestock and to relieve the heifers' heavy udders. The baby was sleeping in the cradle Uncle Silas had made and had carved with her name—*Julia*.

The family had greeted the child in fine fashion. Proud Grandmother Dunwoody had determined it was time to call the family together for a proper celebration of her first grandchild— after all, she was nearly four months old! As usual, Nancy, Carol, and Opal had outdone themselves with food for the guests and gifts for the baby, even some treats—a new bonnet and shirtwaist for mother Margaret herself! The exuberant McKinnon clan and Charlotte, with Lydia and Virginia, in exile from Charleston, came bearing presents and enough joy, it seemed, to alleviate Nancy's anxiety, at least for a time.

The conflict up north had been terrible; James had been at Antietam and had seen the bloodiest aggression—so said the newspapers. Nancy longed for any word from him, but Margaret knew Nancy was aware any description James wrote of the bitter events of war was diluted by his concern for Nancy's health. He gave only a faint, insipid picture of the reality of war—a conflict even more intensely cruel, as it pitted neighbor against neighbor and brother against brother. Nancy insisted on keeping abreast of the regiment's actions in the course of the campaigns, but Margaret and Thomas feared current events would have a deleterious effect on Nancy's already fragile state of being.

Closing her eyes and shaking trouble from her mind, Margaret smiled at the thought of how proud Thomas was of his new daughter! He would boast, "She is the brand-new and beautiful image of Nancy and Margaret, with Grandma McNeal's dancing blue eyes." She could have given no more cherished gift to her beloved Thomas than the daughter he sang to sleep each night with his soothing baritone lullabies.

She reached for the white voile baby gown with the delicate sheering and embroidery of pink roses. The fabric was soft and light between her fingers. Matching under slip, bonnet, jacket—her mother must have worked many hours to complete the exquisite creation, which had to be no less than perfect for Grandmother's Julia.

My, how tired I am! thought Margaret, as she returned the items to the sideboard. *Perhaps I will go lie down a bit before the baby wakes up.* She tugged her leaden feet across the kitchen and through the parlor to their bedroom. She removed the slippers from her feet so as not to disturb Julia, asleep in the cradle by the bed.

Pulling a pillow from under the coverlet, she lay across the bed and placed the cushion beneath her head. She threw her arm over her eyes to shield them from the waning light of afternoon. *How warm it was this late on an autumn day!* Margaret fell into a deep sleep.

Nancy woke from the troubled dreams of James' falling in battle and the screams of the wounded and dying, to hear only the distressed cries of Julia. Moving from her bed and across the keeping room to the open door of the bedroom where Margaret lay, Nancy saw Julia's cries brought no movement from her mother. Nancy hurried to Margaret to see the flush and feel the fire in her cheeks, to see the damp tendrils of loose hair clinging to her neck. Picking up Julia to still her cries, she felt the heat from head to foot in her granddaughter's small body, stiffening with every unceasing wail.

Rushing to the door of the porch, Nancy could see Thomas, pails in hand, heading toward her. Having relieved the cows of their milk, he would pour the milk into the jugs waiting on the porch, cover them with cheesecloth, and set them on the railing to let the cream rise.

"Thomas! Thomas, come quick!"

Thomas mounted the steps in three strides and left the pails unattended on the porch.

May 1863

With the success at Stones River and the stationing of troops at Murfreesboro, Major James Dunwoody requested orders to go to the area with his men, Brady and Allison, then over the plateau toward Chattanooga, to access the integrity of crucial rail lines into the important hub. Plans soon would bring the war to the river terminal city, where rail lines also crossed, East to West and from the North to Atlanta, the prize of the Confederacy. He also asked for a few days' leave to see to the welfare of his wife and family—hopefully, also, to move Charlotte, his daughter, and niece from Chattanooga to the safety and peace of the river house.

Margaret had brought water to Thomas, as he hoed weeds from the garden rows. When his eyes caught the movement of horses coming down the rise to the lane, he nudged Margaret and nodded toward the approaching men in uniform. He dropped his hoe and moved to meet them, as Margaret ran into the house.

James and his men arrived in the yard, dismounted, and James handed the reins of his horse to Allison and pointed to the water trough. "Thomas, my son, you are a welcome sight!"

Thomas moved to wrap his long arms around the officer in blue. "Oh, James, we are so thankful you are alive." Stepping back from the embrace, Thomas added, "If a bit thinner and grayer."

"Thomas, how are our ladies?" James sought Thomas' face for an honest response.

The screen door slammed, and Margaret, supporting a frail but beaming Nancy, walked with her mother toward the waiting men.

"James, my dear James," Nancy said softly. "My prayers have been answered."

James rushed to gather his wife's delicate frame in his arms. He was reminded of a time when he held a baby bird that had fallen from its nest—he felt if he squeezed her, she might crumble. "Nancy, my sweet wife. I have missed you terribly."

"But, now, you are here, and how thankful I am." Turning to the two soldiers, she asked, "And who are these young men?"

"Corporals Allision and Brady." Each man tipped his hat in response to the introduction. "We have just completed our assignment and now have a few days' leave before we report back to our posts. Allison and Brady will go back to Murfreesboro. I will return to my regiment farther north."

"These will be precious days, James. Thomas, can you see to making a comfortable place for these men to rest?" Nancy asked.

"Surely will. We don't have fancy food to offer, but we can fill you up on what we have."

"Thank you, sir," responded Brady.

"Yes, thank you," added Allison.

"James, I can't believe the sight of your blue uniforms could be so beautiful. There was a time I gladly would have shot the three of you." James was thankful Nancy could still tease him, though her smile and voice lacked vigor. *Yes,* he thought, *these days will be precious.*

* * * * * * * * *

Major James Dunwoody lifted his face to the leaves of the ancient oak tree, rustling, dancing light rays in the breeze above Nancy's grave. He had seen the worst of humanity, in clamoring, soul-wrenching cruelty; and, now, on this knoll, the best of human souls would lie in peaceful rest, beneath the soul-soothing sounds of creation. Perhaps, he had hastened her demise with the anxiety he had caused in going—or, perhaps, it was the excitement of his unanticipated return. Three precious days—it was not enough. But, perhaps, her going had saved her from the burden she would know if the next action cost him his life. Nancy's face, her voice, their joyous time together would be memories to sustain and settle him when civilization itself seemed to be unraveling around him.

Her life had faded to a close as she sat peacefully, putting the final exquisite stitches in a lace bonnet for Sara's Tennie. *How fitting,* James thought. *How completely kind and just.* Now, her existence would be marked by a headstone identifying her resting-place in this tree-shaded patch of land that would be their family cemetery on the banks of the Tennessee. *Would she have wanted to rest next to David?* The thought was fleeting. But where David's life ended, Nancy's new life began. His was the new Nancy—the woman that conquered fear and loss to make a way for herself, with only her talent and the strength of her hands and spirit. She had made him stronger, surer, complete. Whatever lay ahead, he knew he could be victorious—one way or the other.

Carol looked around at the faces paying homage to her friend. *No—more than a friend, a beloved sister.* Thomas draped his arm around Maggie's shoulders, as she held her hand on the mound of her growing abdomen. *How gracious the Giver*, Carol thought, *to give another child to ease the pain.* Measles had taken baby Julia and had left Margaret without hearing. Thomas McNeal had been grounded, strong and sure—Margaret's port in the storm. This baby would be the sun's rays, waking the new day at the end of the tempest.

Sara, spent from weeping, and Josiah stood shoulder to shoulder, their children surrounding them like pickets. They might be Carol's grandchildren—she loved them as her own. Samuel was a reedy sapling, the image of Josiah; Clara was round and rosy as Grandpa Silas; Tillie, darkly beautiful, was like Peggy; Josiah was an incongruous composition of Cherokee features and sparkling blue eyes; and toddler, Tennie, was auburn-haired—Silas's 'little precious.'

Opal, elegant in a hooped emerald green and black-striped taffeta, searched the heavens, while the preacher spoke of life and love, labor and loss. They were only words. The woman resting on the bier and those gathered around her needed no words, heeded no words. Nancy was beyond the realm of voice and grief, hidden in each heart attending the disposition of her remains.

James's family stood at the front of a congregation of friends and respectful associates, who had known and admired Nancy and spoke of her industry, honesty, and courage. *Courage*, Carol thought—*that was Nancy's life*. Her courage was responsible for the life of each family member standing now at her graveside. When suffering and loss shook the dreams from her wakening, she took what was real, made it her own, and found in it the best that might be. Stripped of her home and heritage, she charted a new course in the new nation, her confidence and character drawing others with her along the way—Carol, Sara, even Opal.

Carol stood with her hand on Silas's shoulder—his weeping, like his heart, was open and without shame. Silas was life and breath to her, but Carol knew the next time she stood at a gravesite, it might be that of Silas. The years in the chair had taken their toll on his body; there were days when his quiet smile evinced an inner suffering. But, because of the example of the woman being laid to rest before her, Carol knew when the time of his departure arrived, she would mourn for Silas, then go on—as Nancy had, with thankfulness for the time of making memories.

The preacher closed his remarks. "'Then shall the dust return to the earth as it was: and the spirit shall return unto God who gave it.' Amen." The throng of mourners began dispersing to resume their individual processes of living, while the immediate family remained to attend the burial.

Carol's resolve was strong—until James moved from the head of the grave to place a massive bouquet of red roses on Nancy's casket. Nancy had said their time together had been blissful, interrupted only by the terrible war raging just beyond their mountains. How ironic that, the very day Maggie and Thomas had celebrated their marriage, James' state had declared its secession from the Union, and he was forced to confirm his position—either stay or go with South Carolina.

Nancy had visited the McKinnons while James was away. She had been anxious for James's safety, but she had confided to Carol that she was happier than she had ever thought possible. She regretted all the years she and James might have had—years that she had wasted. But she hoped for more when the bloodshed was over. Had it not been for Nancy's illness, Carol thought, she and James might not have had the time they had. But, had it not been for Nancy's illness, they might have had the time for which she hoped.

The sun's rays glinted on the silver streaking his brown hair, as Major James Dunwoody, hat in hand, the broad chest of his uniform dampened by tears, returned to stand at attention at the head of the casket. At his order, Allison and Brady, acting as pallbearers, released the straps and lowered Nancy's body into the grave.

The earth received its own, while the soul had returned to Him who gave it. The old ones called Him "the Giver," Carol remembered—the Giver and Receiver of life. Kaquoli, Carol, looked around her at the people who had filled her existence with love and purpose, at the final resting place of the one who had been the flowing stream that turned the mill wheel of her life. She looked across the expanse of hillside sloping down to the Tennessee—some said it was the Giver. She had left such notions behind long ago—but, her life had begun along its banks, and there she had come again, with Nancy and with Sara, the sisters of her soul, to find her home and heart—and, yes, her contentment. She looked up toward the sunlight flickering through the leaves of the old oak and felt its warmth on her face.

Postscript

Major James Dunwoody gave his life in heroic military action at Gettysburg, Pennsylvania, July 3, 1863. His body, in common with many under his command, his comrades in arms, was not recovered.

CPSIA information can be obtained
at www.ICGtesting.com
Printed in the USA
LVHW111328030519
616557LV00001B/225/P